Like—Boo, Man.

Life is pretty sweet when you're a ghost. Just ask Robbie and his sister, Dora. They've haunted the same house on Fear Street for one hundred years. Every year or two, a different family takes over the house—and Robbie and Dora get a new batch of people to haunt. Awesome!

But then, Oliver Bowen moves in—and Robbie's troubles begin. Oliver doesn't believe in ghosts! And no matter how hard he tries, Robbie just can't frighten him! But Robbie's not about to give up. He and Dora are gathering up all their energy—and tonight they're going to give Oliver a scare he'll never forget!

Also from R.L. Stine

The Beast®
The Beast® 2

Available from MINSTREL Books

WHY I'M NOT AFRAID OF GHOSTS

A Parachute Press Book

A
MINSTREL®
BOOK

PUBLISHED BY POCKET BOOKS

New York   London   Toronto   Sydney   Tokyo   Singapore

A MINSTREL PAPERBACK *Original*

A Minstrel Paperback published by
POCKET BOOKS, a division of Simon & Schuster Inc.
1230 Avenue of the Americas, New York, NY 10020

WHY I'M NOT AFRAID OF GHOSTS WRITTEN BY
NINA KIRIKI HOFFMAN

ISBN: 0-671-00852-8

First Minstrel Books paperback printing August 1997

10 9 8 7 6 5 4 3 2 1

Cover art by Broeck Steadman

Printed in the U.S.A.

R·L·STINE'S
GHOSTS of FEAR STREET®

WHY I'M NOT
AFRAID OF GHOSTS

I

"**W**ait till I get through with this place." Stocky, dark-haired Oliver Bowen glanced around the attic room. "It's going to be the coolest room I've ever had. You'll see."

He gazed at the cobwebs and old furniture and dust. He peered into shadowy corners. A wide grin spread over his face.

It was excellent!

"I don't know," Shawn Wood murmured.

Oliver glanced at Shawn. Shawn shoved his glasses up on his nose and blinked his blue eyes. His spiky blond hair was so pale, it was almost white. He looked kind of like a rabbit.

"Don't know what?" Oliver asked.

I

Shawn shrugged. "Don't you think it's kind of spooky up here?"

"That's what I like about it!" Oliver declared. He pulled open the top drawer of a fancy old bureau and peered inside. Yup, he thought. This place is full of possibilities.

"I was psyched when I saw your moving vans last week," Shawn told him. He hopped on top of an old trunk. "It's been a while since any kids my age lived in this house."

Oliver opened the bottom drawer of the bureau. "You're eleven, right? Like me. So we should be in the same grade," he called over his shoulder. "How come I haven't seen you at Shadyside Middle School?"

"I go to private school," Shawn replied.

"Oh." Oliver nodded. Too bad. Even though he did look like a rabbit, Shawn seemed pretty cool. It would have been fun if they had classes together.

The school term had just started. That made it a little easier. At least Oliver didn't have to start in the middle of the year. But still, most of the kids at Shadyside Middle School had been together since kindergarten.

He sighed. Sometimes it was tough, always being the new kid.

"So you really like it up here?" Shawn asked in a doubtful voice.

"Definitely. I love all this old furniture." Oliver ran his hand along the bureau's carved edges. "You never

2

know where you'll find a secret drawer. Or what you'll find inside!"

Shawn shook his head. "Like a dead mouse? No thanks."

Oliver fiddled with a large standing mirror in the corner. He tilted it first one way, then another. "The last house didn't have cool stuff like this," he declared. "No attic either."

"How many new houses have you had?" Shawn asked.

"Lots." Oliver shrugged. "We move all the time because of my dad's work."

"How come? What does he do?"

"He's a consultant," Oliver explained. "He does stuff for the government."

He strolled over to an old desk and tugged the handle of the rolltop, trying to open it. "I took one of the downstairs bedrooms until I can get this attic fixed up. The farther away from my sister, Nell, the better. She's seven, and she is such a pain! She never stops snooping. Dad says I can put a lock on the door at the bottom of the stairs. Once I do, she won't be able to come up here unless I let her. Which I won't!"

"Want to bet?" Nell's voice floated up the stairs.

"Get out of here!" Oliver shouted at his little sister.

He should have known she'd be listening. What a pest! Sometimes Oliver thought Nell's mission in life was to annoy him. She seemed to be right behind him every time he turned around.

3

"This room is creepy," Shawn muttered. "This whole house is creepy!" He hopped off the trunk. "Listen, Oliver. There's something you should know. There are a lot of ghosts in this town. Especially here on Fear Street."

"Ghosts?" Oliver repeated. He watched Shawn pace around the attic. "You're kidding, right?"

Shawn pointed toward the round, dust-streaked window. "You know the cemetery down the street? People are always running into ghosts there. There used to be a ghost named Pete who controlled people's bodies at night." Shawn shivered. "And I've heard of worse things!"

"Are you nuts?" Oliver asked, wrinkling his forehead. "Or are you just trying to scare me? Because I hate to tell you, it won't work."

"I'm serious," Shawn insisted. "You have to be careful around here. Ghosts are all over the place!"

Oliver grinned. Ghosts were all over Shawn's brain anyway!

Shawn glanced around as if checking for people listening in. "Just about every house on Fear Street has a ghost in it," he whispered. "I bet *this* house has more than one! Nobody's ever lived here longer than a couple of months. This very room is probably haunted!"

Oliver laughed. "Come *on*, Shawn. Don't be demented! Everyone knows there's no such thing as ghosts! Those are just stories to scare babies with. Nothing scares *me*."

"Don't laugh!" Shawn cried. He looked over his shoulder, then whipped his head around to check the other direction. "You'll just make them mad. We'd better get out of here!"

Was Shawn serious? Oliver wondered. If it was a joke, he was putting on some show.

"Get real," Oliver said. "What do you think will happen if I laugh?"

He stepped to the center of the attic. He placed his hands on his hips. "Ha!" he laughed loudly. "Ha! Ha! Ha!"

He heard a rustling noise behind him.

Shawn glanced that way. His eyes widened. "Oh, no," he murmured.

What was he staring at?

Oliver whirled to look behind him.

Something moved near the open window.

Something pale. An old sheet draped across an armchair.

Oliver stared as it rose slowly into the air!

2

Oliver gazed at the sheet hovering above the arm-chair. It curved over something round, its hem flapping in and out.

Shawn lifted a shaking hand and pointed. "L-look!"

Oliver snorted. "Chill, Shawn. It's just Spooky."

Oliver's big black-and-tan Doberman, Spooky, followed him everywhere. Spooky liked to hide under things.

Oliver went over and jerked the sheet from the air above the armchair.

There was nothing below it but an ordinary seat cushion!

Weird, Oliver thought. He glanced around. "I could

have sworn he was under here. Spooky? Where *is* that dumb dog?"

Shawn stared at the sheet. His eyes behind his glasses were wide. "If Spooky didn't make the sheet rise, what did?"

"It was probably just a breeze or something." Oliver waved at the open window beside the chair.

"I've never seen a breeze that could do that," Shawn mumbled. Then he gazed straight at Oliver. "It was ghosts," he declared.

"No way! Anyway, suppose there are ghosts, which there aren't. Why would they make a sheet rise in the air? What a dumb trick!"

"Ghosts don't have to have human reasons for doing what they do," Shawn argued.

"If I were a ghost, I'd pick something way cooler than sheets to play with," Oliver said. He headed for the stairs. "Hey, I've got something to show you in my room. At least, I hope it's still in my room." He raised his voice so his sister would hear. "Which it should be, unless Nell took it."

"I haven't been in your room today!" Nell yelled from below.

"Soundproofing, that's what I really need up here," Oliver muttered as he and Shawn bounded down the creaky attic stairs.

The attic was silent and still for a moment. Dust settled on the floor and on the sheet.

Then twin whirlwinds began to spin, lifting spirals of dust. *Whoosh!* The columns of air swirled faster and faster. The cobwebs stirred in the breeze they gave off.

Slowly, in the middle of the dust tornadoes, two ghostly figures appeared.

3

Robbie coughed. He hated the appearing-as-a-whirlwind trick. It always made him feel dry and thirsty—even though ghosts never needed to drink.

But his older sister, Dora, liked it. And if she felt like doing it, she made Robbie do it too.

They'd been dead more than a hundred years and she was still just as bossy as she used to be when they were alive!

Robbie glanced over at his sister. She looked like an ordinary blond-haired, blue-eyed twelve-year-old girl, her hair in two braids with big ribbons on the ends. She wore an old-fashioned yellow dress with puffy sleeves. No one would guess by looking at her that she was a ghost. Just like him.

"That sheet trick was so dumb!" Robbie complained. "You call that scary? *Babies* wouldn't be scared of that!"

"Some scares work better than others. Babies are scared when they see your hideous face," Dora retorted.

Robbie stuck his tongue out. Then he made the flesh melt off his face until only skull, tongue, and eyeballs were left.

"Much less scary than your regular face," Dora scoffed. "You want to see *scary?*"

Her skin slowly peeled off her whole body, evaporating into the air. She threw her skull back and waved her white bone hands in the air. Then she danced around the attic as a clattering skeleton. Her yellow dress hung from her dry bones.

Robbie had to admit she looked gruesome. It was a really cool trick.

Plus she made her shoes stay on! They were button-up boots. How does she do that? Robbie wondered. Why don't her bones slip right out of them?

Dora danced over to the big dusty mirror in the corner and floated up so she could see herself in her bones. She curtsied to her skeleton reflection, clacking her jawbone.

Robbie shuddered. He hated that noise. Except when *he* did it.

Dora laughed. Her skin rolled over her bones, and she turned back into herself. As she admired herself in the mirror, Robbie came up behind her.

"How come you're always staring at your ghost self?" Robbie asked. "Your face stays the same!"

"Yeah!" Dora replied. "I always look good!" She stuck her tongue out at him in the mirror. "And you always look dumb!" She ruffled his hair, making it stand straight up.

"Cut it out!" Robbie snapped. He smoothed down his blond hair. It was short on the sides and long on top. Then he straightened out his shirt. He wore a navy blue sailor suit with a wide square collar. He hated that suit. But he always appeared in it, because he was wearing it when he died.

That was one of the reasons he liked doing sound effects better than appearing in his natural form. Who could be scared of a ten-year-old kid in a sailor suit?

Dora turned and pushed him away. "Get out of my mirror before you crack it!" she ordered.

Robbie floated over to the desk. He perched on top of it. He *wished* he could crack mirrors! But no.

Dora drifted over to sit on the armchair.

"That Oliver kid is going to be tough," she announced. "I don't want him up here in our attic."

"Neither do I," Robbie said, though he wasn't really sure. He kind of liked Oliver. He seemed fun. And he had lots of cool stuff in his room. Stuff Robbie had never seen before.

"Some dumb lifer getting in the way when we're fixing up a scare," Dora grumbled. She called all

11

living creatures "lifers." "We'd have to watch every move we made!"

"It *is* easier to haunt the house when we can hide in the attic between scares," Robbie agreed. Ghosts didn't have to eat or sleep, but they needed rest sometimes. Especially if they did hard tricks, like moving things or touching people.

"And he's got some nerve," Dora went on. She copied Oliver's tone. " 'Everyone knows there's no such thing as ghosts!' "

Her blue eyes took on a nasty gleam. "Maybe we should show him just how wrong he is," she suggested with a grin.

"Let's scare him," Robbie suggested. "Let's scare him right out of the attic!"

Dora rubbed her hands together. "Better than that! Let's make him run to his parents and beg to move away!"

Move away? Robbie thought. How come she always wants everybody to move away? There's nothing to do around here unless someone is living in the house!

On the other hand, scaring people was what Robbie liked to do best. He couldn't resist a good scare session. "Bet I can scare him better than you can!"

"Bet you can't!" Dora retorted.

"Bet I can!"

"Oh, yeah?" Dora sneered. "Oh, yeah? Well, we'll just see about that! We'll take turns scaring him. The one who makes him run to Mommy and Daddy first wins!"

What a great idea, Robbie thought. A contest!

"Deal. But it's my turn next," he said. "You already tried that stupid sheet trick."

"All right," Dora grumbled. "Whatever you do, I'll top it!"

Stairs creaked behind them.

Robbie jumped. He and Dora whipped around.

Robbie clutched Dora's arm.

His mouth opened and closed.

He couldn't tear his eyes away from the horrible thing he saw!

4

Oliver's little sister, Nell, stood at the top of the stairs.

She stared straight at the ghosts!

Robbie stared back, frozen. Oh, no! he thought. She's not supposed to know about us yet.

This could wreck everything!

How did that kid sneak up on us? We aren't ready to be seen!

Did he and Dora lose their special power to choose when they wanted to appear and to whom?

Or—did this kid have the Sight?

People with the Sight can see ghosts—whether the ghosts want them to or not.

People with the Sight are a ghost's biggest fear. A ghost's worst nightmare!

Robbie stared at Nell. She was small for her age, like her brother. She had short, curly dark hair and dark brown eyes.

"Thunder!" Nell called. "Where are you, you bad cat?"

Whew!

She wasn't looking *at* them, Robbie realized with relief. She was looking *through* them. Looking for her cat!

He took a deep breath, even though he didn't need to breathe anymore. Sometimes it just felt right. He let out a faint sigh.

"Here, kitty kitty kitty," Nell said.

She edged into the room. She chewed on her lower lip and glanced around. She seemed nervous.

Robbie bet *she* would be easy to scare!

"Kitty?" Nell murmured, venturing farther into the room. She studied the sheet on the chair, then the big mirror.

She peeked under the chair, lifting the sheet. "Kitty?"

She searched behind the mirror. "Kitty? Are you up here?"

Then she headed over to the carved wooden rolltop desk that used to be Robbie's when he was alive. The one he was sitting on right now!

Robbie jumped up and floated away from Nell. He hovered in the air above the desk.

Nell rolled up the top of the desk and started opening the little drawers in back of it.

Hey. What was she doing?

Just plain snooping!

No way could a cat fit in any of those drawers!

Now she was humming! She wasn't even calling the cat anymore.

Had she ever *really* been looking for it? Or was she just looking for an excuse to come up here?

Maybe Oliver was right about this kid being a brat.

Nell found Robbie's old magnifying glass and took it out of its drawer. She examined her fingertips through it. Then she stuck it in her pocket.

She's stealing it! Robbie thought, outraged.

What if she found the puzzle drawer where he hid his most excellent secret stuff? His lucky arrowhead, the bullet he found at a Civil War battle site, and the 1894 Liberty Head silver dollar his father gave him on his tenth birthday?

Robbie puffed up. He was going to scare Nell right out of her pink pom-pommed socks!

"Boo!" Dora shouted behind him.

Robbie jumped. He totally lost his concentration.

Nell gasped. She ran downstairs.

"What are you doing?" Robbie yelled at Dora. He hated it when she startled him! *"I* was going to scare her."

"It didn't take much," Dora commented.

Robbie glared at her. "I'm going down to check out

16

Oliver's room now. You better not scare him before I do, or *you automatically lose the contest!"*

Robbie lurked in the doorway of Oliver's room.

Shawn perched on the desk chair, leafing through some comic books. Oliver sat on his bed, playing a weird-looking guitar.

It didn't look like any of the guitars Robbie remembered seeing while he was alive. It was flat instead of hollow, and it was made out of some shiny red stuff that didn't look like wood. It had black knobs on it. Also, it made hardly any sound.

Robbie remembered seeing guitars like Oliver's on televisions that had been in the house before. The families who owned the televisions never stayed in the house long, which frustrated Robbie. He loved TV.

Dora always wanted people to move out pretty soon after they moved in. Lifers irritated her.

Robbie thought that was stupid. The rules of haunting said you could haunt only people who lived under your roof. Or people who were *connected* to people who lived under your roof. So when nobody lived here, who was there to haunt?

People were much more fun to play with than spiders and bats and rats.

Wait a second! What's wrong with me? Robbie scolded himself. I should be coming up with a really good scare!

Back to business. What can I use here in Oliver's room to scare Oliver into believing in ghosts?

Robbie scanned the room. A big black three-ring binder decorated with green lightning bolts sat on the desk. A zip pouch full of sharp new pencils and a package of filler paper lay next to it. There was a stack of textbooks on the desk too.

A computer sat on the desk. The monitor had fish swimming across it.

A glass-sided tank sat by the window. Dirt, a geranium plant, and a bowl of water were inside.

Robbie drifted closer. He peered through the glass.

Yikes! A giant hairy red-legged spider stared back at him!

A tarantula!

What kind of kid had a tarantula for a pet?

Robbie hated spiders.

"So—do you play any instruments, Shawn?" Oliver asked.

Robbie jumped. Did Oliver have to talk so loud?

Shawn shook his head. "Nope. Mom made me take piano lessons when I was nine, but I hated them."

"Too bad. I want to start a band." Oliver carefully placed the guitar on the floor.

Robbie wished the old piano were still downstairs. He used to take piano lessons too, and he liked to play.

He bet Oliver wouldn't know any of the songs he knew though.

Robbie hadn't had many opportunities to listen to current music. People moved out of the house way too fast, and they took their radios and TVs and CD players with them.

Still, he was sure he could learn a new song easily. He was sick of the old ones he knew. And it would be cool to be in a band.

I'm doing it again! Robbie thought. Thinking about making friends with some dumb lifer! Being a traitor to ghosts!

If the piano were still here, I could use it to scare Oliver, Robbie told himself. That's what I *should* be thinking about!

He peeked over Shawn's shoulder to check out the comic book. All he saw were lots of people in weird masks and underwear.

Funny papers sure had changed since Robbie was alive.

Just as Robbie leaned in for a closer look, Shawn clapped the comic book shut and put it on the floor. Frustrated, Robbie drifted toward the door.

"Got any bright ideas, little brother?" Dora asked, appearing right in front of him. "Or are you just mooning around as usual?"

Robbie narrowed his eyes and glared at his sister. He wished he had an idea, but Oliver's room hadn't inspired him.

Aside from the tarantula and some dirty clothes, there wasn't anything scary in Oliver's room.

"Woof! Woof woof woof!"

At the sudden noise, Robbie shrieked and jumped two feet in the air.

He whirled to see a huge black Doberman pinscher leap up from under a pile of dirty laundry.

"Ruff ruff *ruff!*" The dog stood, head forward. It growled low and deep in its throat. Its teeth were huge and white, glistening with saliva.

It stared straight at Robbie!

If Robbie's heart still worked, it would have been pounding.

Before Robbie could even think to move, Spooky lunged right at him!

5

"**N**o!" Robbie shrieked. He shut his eyes in terror.

Then the dog jumped right *through* Robbie, barking like crazy.

Robbie yelled and clutched his stomach.

"Ohh! Ooooch!" he groaned. Yuck! A lifer going through a ghost really made the ghost sick. The ghost's energy got all churned up.

"Spooky, cut it out!" Oliver yelled at the dog.

But Spooky ignored him.

"Woof! Ruff! Rrrrr!" The dog hit the hall running, his nails clicking on the wood floor.

Still gasping, Robbie turned to watch the dog.

"Meorrow!" A big fluffy orange-and-white cat tore down the hall. Spooky charged after it.

21

"Thunder!" Nell wailed, popping out of her room. "Oliver, you better make Spooky stop!"

"Thunder?" Robbie murmured.

Of course. The dog was after Nell's cat. Not the ghosts.

I'd get lost again quick if I were that cat, Robbie thought. As big as the cat was, the dog was *huge!* And fast.

Robbie groaned. His stomach hurt so much, he wished he could just hurl and get it over with. If only ghosts could throw up.

Dora hovered near the ceiling, smirking. She must have moved fast enough to get out of the way of the dog's charge.

"Smooth moves," Dora taunted.

"The dog surprised me," Robbie protested. Yeah. That was it. The dog surprised him.

That wasn't the same as scaring him.

"Look out, Robbie!" Dora teased. "I'm coming down. I don't want to *surprise* you!" She began laughing.

Robbie glared at her as she drifted down from the ceiling to the floor. She was laughing so hard, tears came out of her eyes.

"Oh, you're so good. You're so *scary!*" she yelped. She laughed so hard, she drummed her feet on the floor. "Oh, you're—you're such a *ghoul!*" She floated out of Oliver's room into the hallway, giggling the whole time.

"Shut up! Just shut up!" Robbie charged up the hall, so mad, he forgot his stomachache.

He ran right through Dora! Which he immediately regretted. Their ghost energies got all stirred and snarled up.

Dora lay on the floor and moaned.

Oh, well.

At least she wasn't laughing anymore.

"Here's what I'm going to do," Robbie announced. They were back up in the attic and feeling better. "I'll groan and howl after he's asleep. He'll wake up with nightmares!"

"You groan like a sick cow," Dora commented.

Robbie bristled. Of all ghost tricks, he was best at sound effects. "Oh, yeah? *You* sound like a dying cat."

"Oh, yeah? We'll just *see* who's the best groaner." Dora stood up straighter, took a huge breath, and let out a series of truly awful groans.

It sounded to Robbie as if she were lying deep inside a dark, dank cave. She even got her groans to echo.

Robbie had to admit, she was good.

But he couldn't let her know she had impressed him. She was bossy enough already!

"That's nothing," he said. He was determined to do a better groan. Then she would *have* to say something nice. "Listen to this!"

He started with the low, terrified moan of a person

who's going home after dark and sees a big shadow coming after him. Then he raised it to the shivery mid-moan of someone who can't run any faster. Finally, he lifted it into the shriek of horror as the shadow catches up to the person.

For a second Dora looked like she might say something nice. Then she said, "Not even a sick cow. Sick calf!"

"Oh, come on!" Robbie flopped to the floor in frustration.

Dora took another turn moaning. It sounded to Robbie like the moan of someone whose body was covered with giant squirming, slimy slugs.

She cut off the moan with a slippery gurgle. As though one of the slugs had crawled into her mouth!

"Pathetic," Robbie sneered. He groaned and moaned the way he imagined someone would whose toes and fingers were being nibbled off by rats.

Then he groaned louder, as if the rats were eating their way up his legs and arms.

He ended with one of his trademark hair-raising shrieks.

Dora started moaning again before Robbie even finished.

Pretty soon they were both howling so loudly, they couldn't even hear each other.

Robbie didn't care. It felt good to moan and groan and howl, even if no one was listening. It was fun. Sometimes it got very boring being a ghost.

He and Dora stopped groaning. They grinned at each other.

"I don't know about you," Robbie declared, "but I'm ready for tonight!"

Robbie wished bedtime would hurry up. He couldn't wait to put his plan into action. But the evening seemed to drag on forever. After dinner Oliver and Shawn watched horror movies on TV. So Robbie and Dora watched them too—invisibly.

On the TV set Frankenstein's monster lurched toward terrified villagers in Transylvania.

"How come you like horror movies so much, when you don't even believe in ghosts?" Shawn asked Oliver.

Oliver shrugged. "They're cool."

"I like pretending I'm the monster," Shawn said. He hunched his shoulders, lifted his arms, let his hands flop down at the ends. Then he moaned.

Robbie stared at the back of Shawn's head. What an eerie sound the kid made! It was the sound of someone alone, scared, and in pain. The kid could go pro!

Robbie sneaked around and peered at Shawn's face.

Shawn's eyes glowed behind his red-framed glasses, and his jaw had dropped. He looked brainless and scary. And somehow bigger.

Weird.

Oliver studied his friend. "Awesome," he murmured. Shawn looked pleased.

The next movie, about a giant crawling eye, scared Robbie. He hid in the wall so Dora couldn't see his knees knocking.

"Buck-buck-buck-buck-buck," Dora squawked.

What is she doing? Robbie wondered. He peeked out from his hiding place.

"Buck-buck!" Dora flapped her elbows like chicken wings. "You are such a chicken, Robbie! Look at these guys. They're not scared at all!"

Robbie glanced over at Oliver and Shawn. Oliver wolfed down microwave popcorn. Shawn snuck pieces of popcorn to Spooky, who was pretty sneaky about eating it.

They all stared at the screen. Even Spooky.

Occasionally Oliver or Shawn said, "That's so dumb." "That's so stupid!" "No one would do that!" "This is the lamest movie on the planet!"

But they didn't turn off the TV until the very end of the movie.

Shawn left after the eyeball movie. Then Oliver went upstairs, brushed his teeth, and climbed into bed.

Robbie waited until Oliver's breathing slowed into sleep.

It was time to put his plan into action. He would use all his classics!

First he tuned his voice so lifers could hear him.

He coughed a couple of times to clear his throat. Then he launched into the groan of a man seeing a dead, rotting body for the first time. Kind of a this-is-so-horrible-I'm-going-to-barf groan.

He thought about Spooky jumping right through him and groaned some more, remembering how much his stomach hurt.

Oliver didn't stir. His breathing stayed steady.

Robbie moved closer to the bed.

He moaned the moan of somebody in a haunted house, faced with dozens of ghostly skeletons and rotting corpses, waving loose arms and legs and bones. *Wooooaaaagggghhhhh!*

No reaction from Oliver.

Robbie shook his head. This kid could sleep through a train wreck!

Robbie imagined something huge and scary appearing in front of him out of the darkness. When he had cranked his fear up to maximum, he shrieked.

A beautiful, high-pitched shriek. Sharp as a knife.

Oliver never even twitched!

Robbie took a huge breath, then let out his best wall-shaking, floor-rumbling, black-cat-screeching groan, driving it up and up into a howl that ended in a shuddering scream of terror.

Oliver sat up straight in bed.

Robbie smiled.

Finally! It was working! Nobody could ignore Robbie's best groan!

Wait a second.

Oliver was just sitting there. His eyes were still closed.

Was he sleepwalking? Robbie wondered. Or sleep-*sitting*? Was he even scared at all?

Better make sure. Robbie started another groan.

Oliver's eyes opened. Wide.

Yes!

"I did it!" Robbie yelled. "I scared him. I win!"

6

Yes! Robbie cheered silently. Dora couldn't scare Oliver. But I sure did!

He watched gleefully as Oliver jumped out of bed and ran into the hallway.

Robbie followed, grinning. For years and years Dora had been dancing around in her bones, taunting him with all the scares she could do that he couldn't.

This was so sweet!

Robbie scampered down the hall after Oliver, posing like a muscle man, flexing first his right bicep, then his left.

Oliver dashed to the master bedroom. He threw open the door.

"Mom? Dad?" Oliver called from the doorway. "Dad?"

No doubt about it. Robbie had won the contest!

"What is it, son?" a grumpy voice mumbled from the bed.

"Dad, Nell's having one of her nightmares again," Oliver explained. "She's moaning and groaning."

"What?" Robbie cried.

Nell? Nightmares?

What was Oliver talking about?

"Poor kid," Mrs. Bowen murmured.

"Guess we'd better check on her," Mr. Bowen said.

With yawns and groans, Oliver's parents got out of bed. They followed Oliver back down the hall to Nell's room. Robbie drifted along behind them, all his triumph washing out of him.

Mr. Bowen listened at the door. "I don't hear anything."

"Maybe she woke up," Oliver suggested. "The moaning was real loud just a couple of minutes ago."

Mrs. Bowen turned the door handle, and they all crept into Nell's room.

Robbie hung his head in despair. He felt terrible!

Robbie's classic moans, his awful groans, his piercing shrieks—Oliver thought they came from a little whimpering kid with nightmares?

What a big fat failure!

"I thought she grew out of those nightmares," Mrs. Bowen said, sitting on the bed next to Nell. She touched Nell's cheek. "Honey? You okay?"

"I'm fine," Nell murmured in a sleepy voice. "What's wrong?"

"Were you having a nightmare?" Mrs. Bowen brushed Nell's hair out of her face.

"Kind of. There were weird noises in my dream."

"Are you okay now?" Mr. Bowen asked.

"Sure." Nell yawned behind her hand.

"You sure showed me." Dora's voice behind him made Robbie jump.

He *wished* she would stop doing that!

Dora hovered right behind him and giggled. "That was so scary, Oliver thought he was hearing his itty-bitty little sister!" she gloated. Then she burst out laughing.

"Oh shut up," Robbie muttered.

He dragged himself back up to the attic, feeling miserable.

"You are such a loser," Dora teased. She danced across the floor, up the wall, and all over the ceiling. "Loser!"

She wore a totally smug grin. She hung upside down, which made her smile even worse. "The tiniest of the whiny! The whimpiest of the impy!"

Holding her skirts, she skipped back and forth on the attic ceiling. "You'll feel even stupider when *my* plan works!" she announced.

Oh, no! What if Dora came up with something really cool?

"What are *you* going to do?" Robbie asked.

If *her* scare worked, she would be impossible to live with! She would gloat. And call him names. And laugh at him.

And there was no way he could get away from her. They were stuck here in this house with each other. Forever!

Her next plan better not work.

What could it be?

Maybe he could sabotage it.

No! He wasn't supposed to think like that.

They haunted the house *together*.

They might insult each other for decades, but they weren't supposed to get in each other's way. Not when the goal was to scare a lifer! Ghosts were supposed to work together on hauntings.

"What's your plan?" Robbie asked again.

Dora smiled her killer grin.

"You'll see," she promised. "And watch out. It will scare the afterlife out of you!"

7

Oliver and Mike Conway strolled down the school steps together after their last class. Mike's all right, Oliver thought. But he sure talks nonstop.

"I'm not kidding, Oliver," Mike was saying. He shoved a clump of red hair out of his eyes. "I've definitely met one ghost, and I've heard about some others."

Oliver shook his head. All the kids in this town were like Shawn, he thought. Obsessed with ghosts!

"I've lived in a lot of different towns," Oliver remarked. "But I've *never* met so many kids who believe in ghosts."

"You'll believe too," Mike warned. His face grew pale under his freckles. He glanced around and lowered his voice. "Sooner or later, you'll believe too."

"Well, uh, thanks for the warning," Oliver mumbled at last. He wasn't sure what to say. Ghost stories didn't scare him. But he was the new kid. He didn't want to get off to a bad start.

"No problem." Mike nodded. "Just thought you should know."

Oliver and Mike turned onto Fear Street and headed in opposite directions. Mike's family lived in a house that was also the Shadyside Museum of History's Mysteries. Mike said it was full of stuff like mummies and suits of armor. Oliver thought it sounded cool.

Oliver glanced down the block to his new house. It looked pretty good, considering how broken-down some of the others were.

The big old house was gray with white window frames. A wide porch wrapped around two sides. Lots of lacy pieces of wood edged the roof, and there was a balcony on the top of the house. You reached it through a set of glass doors.

Oliver squinted. If he did it just right, the house looked a little like the one in *The Munsters*. Just the kind of house a kid could explore for hours. Dig up good secrets.

Oliver caught a glimpse of Shawn's pale hair shining on the porch. Shawn was waiting for him again. Good!

The kids Oliver had met in school were friendly enough, Oliver supposed. But he and Shawn had already discovered they liked the same comics and movies and games. And Shawn was funny.

So what if he had ghosts on the brain. All the kids at school did too!

Oliver shrugged off his backpack and pulled out his Frisbee. He always carried it with him. It was pretty chewed up from all the times Spooky had fetched it. But it still flew okay.

"Hey, Shawn!" Oliver yelled, darting toward the house. "Think fast!" He tossed the Frisbee.

Shawn glanced up. He jumped to his feet and reached for the Frisbee. It soared just over his fingertips.

"Oops!" Shawn shrugged and smiled. He raced to the side of the house to get the Frisbee out of the bushes. Then Oliver heard him yell.

Oliver dashed over. Shawn was staring up at one of the attic windows.

"What?" Oliver asked, joining him. "What's the matter?"

"I saw someone up there. In the attic window." Shawn pointed.

"Who?" Oliver stared at the windows. They looked dark and empty.

"In the left window. A face. Watching us!"

Oliver shaded his eyes with his hand, trying to see better. "There's no one there now," he said.

"I saw someone," Shawn insisted.

"So? It was probably just snoopy Nell." Oliver

glanced sideways at Shawn. What's the big deal? he wondered.

"What if it wasn't?" Shawn stooped and picked up the Frisbee. He handed it to Oliver. Oliver noticed Shawn's hand trembling. "What if it's something worse than Nell?"

Oliver shook his head. Obviously, Shawn didn't have an annoying younger sister.

"What could be worse than Nell, the biggest brat in the universe?" he asked. "She snoops. She eavesdrops. She tags along. She bosses. She eats my desserts, and she steals my coolest stuff. She's the worst!"

"What if it were a ghost?" Shawn asked.

Man, did Shawn have a one-track mind. "What *is* it with you and ghosts?" Oliver demanded.

Shawn chewed on his lower lip. "Look, I have to ask you something, and this time I'm serious. Do you believe in ghosts, even a little bit?"

Oliver frowned. "Why do you want to know?"

"Because—" Shawn began.

"Hey, Oliver!" someone yelled.

Oliver turned to see Nell strolling up the sidewalk.

"Don't you think school is way easier here?" she shouted. "Aren't you glad we moved here?"

"I would be glad if we moved somewhere else and left you behind," Oliver muttered so only Shawn could hear.

But Shawn wasn't listening. "Uh, Oliver?" he murmured. His pale blue eyes were wide. He sounded scared.

"What's wrong?" Oliver asked.

"If Nell's out here," Shawn whispered, "then who was that in the window?"

8

Oliver stared up at the window. He still didn't see anything. He glanced at Shawn. "Are you *sure* you saw something?" he asked.

"I'm sure!" Shawn insisted.

"Maybe it was just the curtain blowing around," Oliver suggested.

"It was a face," Shawn sputtered.

"I guess it could have been my dad," Oliver offered. "He's working in his home office today. I guess he might have gone up to the attic for something."

"No!" Shawn shook his head violently. "It was a girl's face. I'm telling you!"

Oliver tried to think of something to say to calm Shawn down. "The curtain could have looked like a girl's face. People mistake things for other things all the time."

"But—"

"Hey!" Nell interrupted, stopping in front of Oliver. "You're supposed to fix me an after-school snack, Oliver!"

Oliver flipped the Frisbee and caught it. Nell was right. Fixing her something to eat was his after-school chore.

"I'm hungry! Feed me!" She tried to chomp Oliver's arm.

He yanked his arm away. She could be so annoying! Especially in front of his friends.

"Feed me *now!*" Nell opened and shut her mouth, making smacking noises with her lips.

"Quit it!" Oliver ordered. He bonked Nell on the head with the Frisbee.

"I'll quit it. But only if you make me cinnamon toast and spread the butter all the way to the edges and put lots of sugar on it. Or I'll tell Mom about—"

"Shut up," Oliver snapped. He rolled his eyes. "Sorry, Shawn," he apologized. Then he bonked Nell again with the Frisbee. "Come on inside and I'll make you your stupid toast."

"That's your big idea?" Robbie asked Dora in the attic. "Appear in the window? What's so scary about *that?*"

"That wasn't a scare, that was an accident!" Dora snapped. "I was watching for Oliver to come home so I could do my next scare. I didn't mean Shawn to see me. I guess I slipped."

"You have to be more careful," Robbie warned. He enjoyed having a chance to nag her for a change. The way she usually nagged him. "You have to build your scare, not waste your time and talents on dumb not-scary things that don't work."

"Look who's talking! Mr. Moan-athon! Mr. I'm-So-Scary!"

"Shut up!" Robbie yelled. Sometimes Dora made him so mad, he wanted to push her through a wall!

But if he shoved her, and she wasn't solid enough to be shoved, they'd get mixed up again, and that hurt.

"This scare of yours better be amazing," Robbie challenged her. "Or I'll spend the next ten years reminding you how you showed yourself to Shawn when you didn't mean to."

"That's all right," Dora said. "I have a lot more memories I can use on you. Like when the dog popped up out of the laundry. What a scream!"

Robbie hung his head.

She was right! He was a sad excuse for a ghost sometimes.

Robbie watched Oliver slip a shiny disk into the CD-ROM drive of his computer. Shawn and Oliver sat on swivel chairs in front of Oliver's desk.

"I just got this game, Wild World Off-Road Super Rally," Oliver told Shawn. "This one is supposed to be really great!"

Robbie, hovering behind Oliver and Shawn, stared at the computer screen.

He knew Dora was going to do her scare soon. She had told him she would do it during a computer game. Robbie wondered what kind of scare it would be.

He concentrated on the screen. Maybe if he watched very carefully, he could figure out what Dora did and how she did it. Then maybe she wouldn't tease him so much.

Music came from the computer's speakers as the screen went dark. Drums beat. Flutes played. Gradually a scene came up.

Deep, dark jungle.

Robbie shivered. He was getting creeped out already!

A stream ran across the left corner of the screen. The water rushed and bubbled. A black panther crept along a wide branch. It growled, showing white teeth and a red tongue. Then a safari car drove in from the right, and the music cheered up.

Words popped onto the screen one at a time in fat red letters shaded with orange and brown.

A crowd of voices chanted the words as they appeared:

OFF

ROAD

RALLY!

"Yes!" Oliver cried, gripping the joystick. He clicked to start the game.

The view switched to inside the safari car. The screen showed the top of the steering wheel, the dashboard with its dials, and just a little of the car's front hood. The car sped along a rocky dirt road. Robbie could see jungle through the windshield.

Long branches dipped down from trees on either side. Robbie saw a big green snake curled around one. He tried not to shudder. He thought snakes were almost as creepy as spiders.

Oliver pushed the joystick forward. The car bumped over the rocky terrain, with happy music bouncing along. Banana tree branches thwacked the roof of the car, with sound effects.

"Cool!" Shawn exclaimed.

"So when is it going to start to get tough?" Oliver wondered.

A girl suddenly appeared on the track in front of the car.

"What?" Oliver yelped, jerking back on the joystick. The car slowed and stopped.

Wow! Robbie wondered what would have happened if Oliver crashed the fake car into the fake girl.

What kind of game *was* this, anyway?

Wait a second. Wasn't that—?

Dora!

This was it!

This was Dora's scare!

9

Robbie hugged his elbows and hunched his shoulders. What would she do? How had she gotten inside the computer?

He wished he knew how to do stuff like that.

Dora's yellow dress billowed in the breeze. She looked almost alive.

She stood motionless for a moment, then strolled right up to the windshield.

"What? I don't think this game is supposed to work like this," Oliver muttered.

Shawn slid his chair a foot away from the computer.

Dora leaned forward until her face filled up most of the monitor. The car's dashboard disappeared.

She smiled. Slowly.

Knowing Dora, Robbie flinched. He prepared himself to be scared. He knew to expect the worst.

Skin melted off Dora's face, sizzling away, leaving a skull behind.

"Yow!" Shawn cried, backing up some more.

Dora's skull grinned. Then, somehow, she made the grin grow wider. Even without flesh.

"Hello, Oliver," the skull said, and clacked its teeth together. "How do you like *this* game?"

It opened its mouth and flame roared out!

Shawn screamed.

So did Robbie.

Robbie clapped his hands over his mouth. Too late though. Dora heard him for sure!

Oliver stared at the skull as it laughed and smacked its teeth together. Then he jumped out of his chair.

He tore out of the room. "Dad! Dad!" he yelled at the top of his lungs.

Robbie felt terrible. The game was over—and Dora had won.

He watched Oliver run down the hall. Shawn must have ducked out, because he was nowhere in sight. Robbie hadn't seen him leave. But then, Robbie hadn't noticed much while Dora scared him silly.

Dora popped out of the computer and floated around the room, her flesh back on her grinning face. "I win!" Dora announced. "I am the Queen of Fright!"

"Come on," Robbie muttered. Misery made him feel a little sick, but he had to see this through. He headed into the hall after Oliver. "We need to find out what Oliver is going to do."

"Do?" Dora repeated. "As if we don't already know!" She was so happy, she floated on air instead of walking along the ground.

Robbie tried to ignore her.

It was tough to do.

"Hah! Did you see the look on his face?" Dora growled like the panther in the opening sequence of Off-Road Rally. "I am the Scream Supreme!" she yelled.

Oliver didn't head for his parents' bedroom this time. He ran to the big room downstairs, where his father had set up his office. It was filled with all kinds of weird electronic equipment. Robbie still hadn't been able to figure out what Mr. Bowen did with his machines.

Oliver burst into Mr. Bowen's workroom. Robbie and Dora drifted in behind him.

"Dad," Oliver said. "Dad!" Then he stomped around the room.

"What's the matter, son?" Mr. Bowen asked.

"I . . . uh . . . I . . ."

"Say it," Dora whispered. "'I'm scared to death. We have to get out of this nightmare house!' Say it! Say it!"

Oh, please, Robbie thought, don't act scared this time, Oliver. Give *me* another chance to scare you! Don't give Dora the satisfaction!

Mr. Bowen left the room for a minute and came back with a glass of water. He handed it to Oliver.

"You okay?" he said.

Oliver nodded, red-faced, and took a sip of water. "That new game you got me," he began.

"Yes?"

"That dumb game! It started out being this cool off-road racing simulator, but then it went totally buggy. It's all mixed up with some stupid haunted-house game!"

"Huh," Mr. Bowen grunted.

"This girl turned into a skull and made stupid noises," Oliver continued. "What kind of idiot game is that? We must have gotten a defective copy. It's totally dorky."

Idiot game! Dorky! Robbie wanted to laugh out loud.

Oliver wasn't scared.

He was annoyed!

Sometimes Robbie really liked this kid.

"So—can we return it?" Oliver asked.

"Sure, Oliver," Mr. Bowen promised. "I'll take care of it tomorrow."

"Thanks, Dad." Oliver drank the rest of the water and headed back to his room.

"What is wrong with him?" Dora raged as she and

46

Robbie followed Oliver back upstairs. "We knew he was going to be a tough scare, but this is ridiculous!"

Robbie almost snickered. But that would have made Dora madder. She was already mad enough.

"Shawn?" Oliver called as he entered his room. "Spooky?"

The Doberman scrambled to his feet, his tongue lolling from his mouth. Robbie eyed the dog warily. He didn't want to be jumped through again.

Oliver patted the dog's head. "Spooky, where's Shawn?"

"Ruff," Spooky answered.

"Yeah, right," Oliver muttered. "I'm asking a dog. But still. Where did Shawn go? That skull face in the game must have spooked him." He shook his head. "You know, he sure gets scared easy."

"Unlike *some* idiots," Dora muttered.

Robbie hid a smile. It looked as if Dora's big scare had fallen pretty flat.

"Whatever you do, it can't possibly be better than *my* scare," Dora declared when they were back in the attic.

"*Your* scare," Robbie repeated sarcastically. "It worked so well. Hah."

"Hey. I heard you scream!"

Robbie felt as if he were turning red, even though ghosts can't blush. "Well, you just surprised me, that was all."

"You were scared," Dora said. "Admit it."

Robbie gazed at his big sister. "Okay. I was scared. But so what? *Oliver* wasn't. Not even for a second!"

Dora frowned. "For my next scare, I'll try something bigger."

"No fair," Robbie protested. "It's my turn next!"

Dora crossed her arms and smirked at him. "You might as well give up and let me take the next turn. You know you can't come up with anything better than my amazing computer glitch."

"Oh, yeah?" Robbie yelled. "Just wait! Just wait until tonight! I'll give him nightmares so bad, he can't wait to wake up, and when he wakes up, it'll be worse!"

Dora shook her head. "You pale excuse for a ghost! What happened last night? 'My little sister is having nightmares!' What makes you think tonight is going to be different?"

"You'll see," Robbie countered. He was so mad at Dora, he wanted to spit. But ghosts can't do that either. "Just you wait. You'll see!"

He didn't know yet exactly *what* she would see.

But he was going to come up with something huge!

10

Robbie never prepared more carefully for a haunt in his whole afterlife.

But it would be worth it. He had plans. Big plans!

He wished he knew some of Dora's special tricks though. He'd feel more sure of himself.

Never mind. He had plenty of his own tricks up his sailor-suit sleeves!

From his perch on top of Oliver's dresser, Robbie watched Oliver turn out the light and pull up the covers.

Spooky strolled over to the desk. He turned around three times and then lay down.

Robbie didn't start his scare right away. It was always better to begin haunting when people were shaken up and confused.

Waking them out of a sound sleep with wild noises was one of the best ways to shake them up!

Robbie thought over his stunts, rehearsing them in his mind while he waited for Oliver to fall asleep.

This kid sure tossed and turned a lot!

Why did he keep fiddling with his sheet?

Maybe I should go ahead and start now, Robbie thought. Maybe Oliver would be scared enough.

No. Stick to the plan! Robbie scolded himself. He forced himself to wait.

Finally Oliver was breathing long and slow. Robbie drifted above Oliver's bed. Yup! He could hear soft snores. Time for the scare to begin.

Robbie tuned his voice and his sound effects so that only Oliver could hear them. Then he groaned.

Just a little groan to start out. To kind of ease into it. Sneak into Oliver's dreams.

Robbie curled his fingers into claws. He floated over to Oliver's closet and scraped his nails across the wood, making *skritch*ing noises. The sound of skeletons trying to dig through your closet door to get you.

Robbie touched the door hinges with ghost fingers. Creak! Creeeek! Rusty hinges, opening slowly . . . slowly . . .

To let in the night things!

Robbie called up footsteps—to run around Oliver's bed.

Then whispers! The sizzling whispers of creatures planning mischief! Plotting near the bed where a

50

sleeper could *almost* understand what they were talking about—but not quite!

Oliver turned over and sighed in his sleep.

Fine. Robbie was just warming up!

Hmmmm. What next? Ah! Owl hoots. First far away, then coming closer.

Now heavier footsteps. Clomp clomp *clomp clomp!* The Frankenstein monster, stomping and stumbling his way here.

Then a frightful, long moan.

Oh, yes! All the good stuff!

The howls of a whole pack of wolves under a full moon.

Just setting the scene!

Robbie summoned ghost chains. He shook them once and listened to the sound they made, links hitting each other. Clash, jingle, clink!

Nice.

Robbie rattled the chains harder! He imagined something chained up because it was too wild and bad to be loose. It ached to escape! It struggled against the chains.

Rattle, clang . . . *snap!*

One chain broke!

Rattle *snap snap snap!*

All the chains burst open!

Thump! Thwop! Something coming! Something with two legs, and . . . swish, swish . . . wings wide enough to brush the ceiling!

It muttered and snorted. "Tasty," Robbie growled in his best monster voice. "Tasty boy! Nice nibble-icious fingers and toes! Nice munchy nose! Yuuuuum!" He tweaked Oliver's nose.

If Robbie had been in the bed, he would have woken up screaming!

Oliver brushed his hand across his nose. His eyes stayed closed, and he still breathed slowly.

He sure was a heavy sleeper!

Robbie glanced around. He knew he was making all these noises himself. But they were so good, he almost expected to see the goblins and skeletons and giant cannibal bats and the Frankenstein monster crowded around the room, leaning over to smile hungrily at Oliver. Their next victim!

Or maybe even stare hungrily at Robbie!

But no, Robbie reassured himself. Nothing else was here.

Just Oliver, asleep in the bed, and Robbie, drifting in the air.

Whew!

Okay. Robbie hadn't pulled out all the stops yet!

Robbie had summoned all kinds of pretend monsters to the room, but they weren't really here.

But I am! Robbie thought with a grin.

Ghosts were real, no matter what Oliver believed. And there was a ghost in here all right!

Robbie moaned. He groaned. He cried out in terror and agony.

"Oh, it hurts. It hurts!" he shrieked. "It's *killing* me! And it's coming for *you!*"

He howled so loudly that the covers of comic books on the floor flipped open and pages fluttered.

He screamed. He gurgled with a horrible wet, choking noise, then stopped as if his throat had been cut.

Oliver lay quietly on the bed below Robbie. So quiet. He wasn't snoring anymore.

Was he even breathing?

Oh, no! What if he wasn't?

What if Robbie had scared Oliver to *death?*

Robbie dropped down and stood on the floor by Oliver's bed. He leaned over to listen.

What if Oliver wasn't breathing?

He'd seen TV shows where people did CPR and brought other people back to life. But he didn't know anything about CPR! He never watched a TV program long enough to learn how to do it!

"Oliver?" Robbie reached out to shake Oliver's shoulder. But he couldn't. He'd used up all his energy on sound effects! His hand went right through Oliver!

Panic rose in Robbie like a scream.

"Oliver?" he whispered urgently. "Please wake up! Oliver? Are you okay?"

Robbie stood frozen beside Oliver's bed. Was Oliver still alive?

Oliver snorted and turned over again. He started snoring.

Oliver wasn't dead.

He was just asleep. Deeply asleep.

Robbie couldn't believe it!

Oliver had slept through the entire haunting!

Every moan, every howl, every creeping, slobbering, *skritch*ing, stumbling sound of it!

All of Robbie's best work!

How *could* he?

Robbie was so mad that if he had had any energy left, he would have tipped Oliver out of bed onto the floor!

That would have done it! Yeah! Tangle him up in sheets and dump him onto the floor!

Why hadn't Robbie thought of that before?

Nothing like a good thud on a hardwood floor to wake somebody up surprised!

But no. Robbie had used up all his energy on sound effects.

What an idiot he was!

"Rats!" Robbie muttered, stomping around the room.

He almost tripped over Spooky.

Even the *dog* slept through Robbie's haunting!

"Boo," Robbie said. Then, enraged, he screamed "Boo!" as loud as he could in Spooky's ear.

"Woof," Spooky mumbled without opening his eyes.

What a waste! What a worthless waste!

"Well, that was as exciting as a Sunday afternoon nap," Dora's snotty voice jeered.

Oh, great. Not only did he use up all his best noises, but now he'd have to listen to Dora gloat!

Robbie headed for the attic. He couldn't stand being in Oliver's room a moment longer. The scene of his miserable failure.

All his best skills. And not one of them had scared his victim.

Robbie felt exhausted as he climbed the attic stairs. He was so tired, he couldn't even float up.

He couldn't remember feeling this tired before.

He began the night with so much energy. Now he had almost zero. He didn't have enough energy to be bothered when Dora danced around the attic, taunting him.

He was too tired to care!

"Mr. High-and-Frighty," Dora teased.

"Cut it out," Robbie moaned. "Just shut up." He slumped in the armchair, so weak, he couldn't even raise dust.

Dora did a little tap dance. "Don't you worry, Mr. Useless-Excuse-for-a-Nightmare!"

"Don't worry? Even *you* can't scare this guy. Nothing works," Robbie mumbled. "We've tried everything we usually do."

Dora grinned. "So it's time for something completely different! A whole new tactic. Guess what? Tomorrow I'm going to follow Oliver to school!"

"School?" Robbie felt stunned. "When was the last time we left the house?"

"Never," Dora admitted. "But this is a special case. Don't you want to get this guy? How could he ignore that last howl of yours?"

Robbie stared at his sister. Had she almost said something *nice* about his haunting?

"Let's scare him out in the open, in front of other kids!" Dora exclaimed.

What a mean plan!

Robbie felt so encouraged, he even managed to smile.

In the morning Robbie watched Oliver and Nell having breakfast.

Robbie was still so tired from haunting the night before, he wished he could eat some Sugar-Frosted Nuggets himself!

Mrs. Bowen stood by the counter, yawning, drinking coffee, and making lunches for the kids.

"Did either of you have any more weird dreams last night?" she asked.

"No," Nell replied.

Robbie tensed, hoping that Oliver would talk about monsters. Ghosts. Bats, wolves, owls . . . anything!

"No," Oliver said. "Not that I remember."

Dumb kid!

Maybe he had no imagination.

Maybe he was too stupid to be scared!

"Oh, wait. There was something about . . . chains . . ." Oliver murmured.

Yes! Robbie perked up. Here it comes!

"Chains?" Mrs. Bowen asked.

"Chains," Oliver repeated. "Rattling chains. I think I was dreaming—about my band! Yeah! Finally an awesome name for my band. The Rattling Chains! I like it!"

No, Robbie thought. No! *No!*

"Don't worry," Dora whispered in Robbie's ear. "Oliver won't be this calm when *I* get through with him."

Robbie nodded. Right now he didn't care *who* scared Oliver. As long as Oliver was really frightened. Then maybe Oliver would finally believe in ghosts!

12

Dora and Robbie followed Oliver and Nell on the way to school, pretending to be their shadows.

Robbie was peeved because Dora shadowed Oliver. She had picked first. So Robbie had to stick with Nell.

He didn't like being a girl's shadow.

It was perfect ghost weather. Dark clouds covered the sky. The wind blew dried leaves along the curbs. The air was cool and smelled like rain.

Nell pulled a pink collapsible umbrella out of her backpack. She pressed the button to open it and held it above her head.

"Put that umbrella down," Oliver scolded. "It's not raining yet."

"I like it up," Nell replied.

Oliver rolled his eyes. "You look dumb."

Nell stuck out her tongue, but she closed the umbrella. "Will you walk me over to this girl Tracy's house after school today?" she asked. "I met her yesterday, and she invited me over."

"Did you check with Mom?"

"Yeah."

"Did you check with Tracy's mom?"

"Yeah."

"Okay," Oliver said. "I'm glad you're making friends. Maybe you'll leave me and Shawn alone now!"

"Hah!" Nell scoffed. "Maybe we'll *both* spy on you!"

"You better not!"

Nell just smirked.

Robbie agreed with Oliver. Nell was a brat!

They reached Shadyside Elementary School. Kids flooded down the street and out of parked cars, heading into the front entrance.

"Be here after school!" Nell commanded before running off. She joined a little girl with pink-framed glasses on the front steps of the school.

Robbie almost shadowed Nell into school. He noticed when she was halfway across the street. He jerked himself loose from her shadow just in time.

"Bossy! For a little kid, she's awfully bossy!" Oliver was muttering as Robbie drifted back.

60

"Wake up!" Dora yelled for Robbie's ears only. "We have a job to do!"

"*You* have a job. I'm just going to watch!"

"All right," Dora growled. "Watch and learn!"

Both ghosts clung to Oliver's shadow as he went inside the big redbrick school. There were so many students in the halls that Robbie was confused. He hadn't seen these many people in one place in a long time! If ever—outside of TV.

Oliver's first class was English. Robbie was relieved to get to a room where they could stay still for a while. It was hard following Oliver when he dodged between people. This school was huge and noisy!

Dora didn't start anything yet. Robbie wondered if something was the matter with her.

Maybe she was just trying to get used to being in this big building! It felt strange to be outside the house.

By the end of Oliver's class, Robbie began feeling better, more himself. Dora seemed to perk up too.

Oliver's second class was math. Robbie had an easier time navigating the halls this time. Dora winked at him, so she must be ready for the big scare.

The teacher, Mr. Gerard, handed out a math test. "Now that we've gotten the introductory material out of the way, I want to see where you all are in math. We have some new faces in Shadyside this year." He smiled at Oliver.

Oliver smiled, looking embarrassed. He peeked at the kids near him. Robbie checked them out too. They were studying Oliver. He was the new kid after all.

"Oh, yeah," Dora murmured. "This will be good. Now everybody's looking at him."

Dora clasped her hands above her head and shook them like a champion. Robbie rolled his eyes.

"Here's an extra sheet of paper," Mr. Gerard continued, passing out blank paper to all the kids. "Remember, show your calculations, everyone!"

Some kids groaned and mumbled that it was too hard, but Robbie noticed Oliver went right at it. Oliver must be good at math.

Oliver was breezing through the third problem when Dora sprang into action. She grabbed the pencil out of his hand. She zoomed up and drilled the pencil point-first into the ceiling.

Oliver blinked, stared at his paper and his hand.

He peered down at the floor.

No pencil.

But also no reaction.

Robbie knew what Dora did wrong. She performed the pencil trick so fast, Oliver didn't even know what had happened!

Oliver yawned into the back of his hand, dragged out his backpack, and pulled out his three-ring binder.

He flipped it open and took another pencil out of the zipped pocket in front. Then he went back to work.

"Do it slower," Robbie suggested. "He has to be able to see where it goes."

"Shut up!" Dora snapped.

But Robbie noticed that she did what he said. For once.

She grabbed Oliver's pencil slowly this time. She waved it around in front of his eyes to make sure he was watching what she was doing, then zapped it up into the ceiling. It hung quivering next to the other pencil.

Oliver stared at the two pencils for a second.

Then he got out another one and went back to work.

Dora's mouth dropped open. So did Robbie's.

"How can he ignore those pencils?" Dora demanded. Robbie shrugged.

Dora tried again. But this time Oliver clutched his pencil so tight, Dora couldn't snatch it away!

"Let go!" she screeched in frustration. Since she couldn't get the pencil away, she jiggled it so Oliver scribbled on his math paper.

He frowned and erased the squiggles.

And went back to work!

By this time, Robbie noticed, other kids were peeking at Oliver. The girl at the desk to Oliver's right sat staring at the pencils in the ceiling, her mouth open. The boy to Oliver's left narrowed his eyes, glancing from the pencils to Oliver and back.

Robbie tried to send a mental message to Oliver. Just act scared, Robbie ordered him. Act scared, and we'll leave you alone!

Oliver ignored the ceiling pencils, the other kids, and Robbie's thoughts, and went on working.

Robbie could tell Dora was really steamed now! She snatched Oliver's notebook off his desk and slammed it onto the floor!

Mr. Gerard looked up. Several heads whipped around.

"Uh," Oliver mumbled. "Sorry."

He leaned over to pick up his notebook. Dora grabbed his third pencil and shot it into the ceiling!

Oliver just got out another one.

Robbie shook his head. How can Oliver stay so calm? he wondered.

The girl next to Oliver gasped. "But—but—" she stammered, pointing at the ceiling.

"What?" Oliver asked. He glanced up. "Oh." He shrugged and gazed back down at his test. He studied the next problem on his paper, chewing on his pencil.

All the kids in the class stared at him. One or two giggled.

The boy to Oliver's left leaned over. "How did you *do* that?" the boy whispered.

64

Yeah, Oliver, Robbie thought, explain that one.

Oliver just smiled mysteriously and went back to work.

The room buzzed as the class muttered and murmured. Some kids pointed at the pencils in the ceiling.

"Class!" Mr. Gerard exclaimed. "What's all this noise? Get back to work!"

The kids stopped whispering. They bent over their math tests. They picked up their pencils and went back to work.

But everyone kept sneaking looks at Oliver.

No one could concentrate!

Dora swooped at Oliver's desk. She grabbed his math test and tugged it.

Oliver dropped his pencil on the desk and grabbed his test. Dora snatched his fourth pencil and jammed it into the ceiling!

Oliver sighed.

"Coo-uhl!" the boy on Oliver's left exclaimed.

Robbie couldn't believe it. All Oliver did was open his notebook and reach into his pencil keeper.

But this time Oliver came up empty-handed.

He glanced at the girl next to him. She shook her head no.

He peeked at the boy to his left. Another head shake.

Oliver sighed again and stood up. He gazed at the

pencils in the ceiling. He climbed onto his desk chair and reached for them.

"Oliver Bowen, exactly *what* do you think you're doing?" Mr. Gerard demanded.

That was when Dora did her worst. Or best, depending on how you looked at it, Robbie thought.

She grabbed Oliver and spun him around on the chair!

Robbie clutched his stomach. Oliver twirled so fast! If *he* were spun like that, he knew he would throw up.

Robbie flew up to the ceiling as the class went wild. Kids jumped to their feet. The whole room buzzed with their exclamations: "Wow!" "No way!" "How does he do that?" "Oh, man!" "Teach me to do that!"

Mr. Gerard tried to restore order. "Oliver Bowen!" he shouted. "Stop that! Oliver Bowen! Do I have to send you to the principal's office? Class! Settle down!" He hit his desk with a steel ruler.

Still the kids pointed, talked, and stared.

Dora spun Oliver six times. Then she let go of him.

Robbie gazed at his sister. She was fading. Her outline was beginning to blur. She used up a lot of energy moving something as big as a boy! She looked a little green.

But what about Oliver? Did Dora's haunting work? Was he afraid? Robbie turned to face him.

Oliver swayed on his chair, trying to steady himself. He opened his eyes really wide.

And his mouth!
His face twisted.
Robbie groaned.
Oliver was going to scream! Robbie just knew it!
Oliver was going to scream in terror!
Dora had won the bet!

13

Oliver's mouth stretched opened even wider.

This was going to be some scream, Robbie thought hopelessly.

And Dora was going to be impossible to live with now!

Then . . .

Oliver sneezed!

"Bless you," the girl to his right whispered.

"Oliver Bowen, explain your behavior!" Mr. Gerard demanded.

Oliver reached up and grabbed all four pencils from the ceiling tiles. Then he jumped down off the chair.

"I'm sorry," he said.

"Sorry doesn't cut it, mister. What were you doing on that chair?"

"I was, uh, going to get my pencils off the ceiling," Oliver explained, "but then I—I—well, I could feel myself about to sneeze. I mean a big one! And trying not to sneeze made me kind of jerk around, and then it got out of control somehow and, uh . . ."

Mr. Gerard glared at him.

"I—"

Mr. Gerard's eyes narrowed.

Robbie hovered over Oliver. What is he going to say?

"I won't do it again," Oliver promised with a little smile.

"See that you don't. You have fifteen minutes to finish this test. I hope you do as well in math as you do in excuses. Class, get back to work!"

"You moron! You dunce! You idiot!" Dora yelled at Oliver, bouncing around him in total frustration. "Don't you even know when you've been haunted? How stupid can you be?"

Oliver didn't even look up.

Who *is* this kid? Robbie wondered. What is with him? He *knows* he didn't spin around like a whirlwind on purpose! Does he really think *he* threw those pencils at the ceiling?

No way! He *has* to know we're haunting him!

Why isn't he scared?

Dora swooped down and grabbed at Oliver's pencil, but her fingers went right through it.

She didn't have enough energy left to do anything!

It was almost sad to see her so low, Robbie thought. He didn't even feel like gloating over her failure.

"Why am I wasting all my talent on a dodo like you?" Dora screamed. "This is ridiculous! Let's go home, Robbie! Let's go home and plan something really big!"

"But I haven't tried anything here yet," Robbie protested.

"What could you possibly do that would be better than what I did?" Dora demanded.

"You mean, what could I do that would be *worse?*" Robbie retorted.

He wished he knew!

He was starting to think there was *nothing* they could do to scare Oliver Bowen. The kid was a rock!

And Robbie sure didn't have enough energy yet to do the kind of fantastic tricks Dora had just done.

But then, even Dora's best tricks hadn't scared Oliver.

What Robbie needed was a totally *different* idea.

He didn't have one yet. But he planned to come up with one.

Very soon!

Robbie didn't have a big idea until science class, later in the day.

He spent the time in between studying Oliver.

Word about Oliver, the pencils, and the spinning

had spread quickly. Kids glanced at Oliver sideways and whispered about him everywhere he went.

Kids asked Oliver how he had done the pencil-in-the-ceiling trick. Others wanted to know how he spun in the chair without falling over. Oliver just shrugged and smiled.

"Can you show me?" a boy asked in the hallway. "I want to add it to my magic act!"

"Maybe later," Oliver replied.

Robbie shook his head. Dora's haunting just gave Oliver something to talk about! It actually made Oliver popular.

Dora seemed stunned by her defeat. She drifted silently beside Robbie. Every now and then she would tug at Robbie's sailor shirt, whining, "Can we go home now?"

Robbie had never seen her so pathetic. Maybe this problem with Oliver had a good side!

Science was the last class of the day.

Oliver took the lab table farthest from the front.

Mr. Gosling, the science teacher, tapped his desk to get everyone's attention. "Okay, folks, find a lab partner," Mr. Gosling instructed.

All the kids paired up. Except Oliver.

There was an odd number of kids in the class. Somebody had to be left out.

Did Oliver mind? Robbie didn't think so. Oliver just smiled.

"Today we're going to learn about Bunsen burners," Mr. Gosling began. "Bunsen burners are ingenious devices, but they can be dangerous because they make a really hot flame. Which is also why they're so helpful. We're going to cook a lot of cool stuff over these little campfires!"

Sounds fun, Robbie thought wistfully.

When he was alive, they never did stuff like this in school!

Mr. Gosling glanced around the room, making sure the class was paying attention. "I want you kids to respect your Bunsen burners," he continued. "Check your lab tables now. Anyone missing a Bunsen burner? Raise your hand if you are."

No one raised a hand.

Robbie drifted closer to study the Bunsen burner.

"Anyone missing a spark striker? Or a pair of safety goggles?"

Again nobody raised a hand.

"Does everybody see that big red fire extinguisher on the wall over there?" Mr. Gosling pointed.

Everyone nodded.

"Okay," Mr. Gosling said. "If things get out of hand, I'm going to grab that and spray you all with white foam. Now watch what I do. Don't do anything yet! Just watch!"

Mr. Gosling demonstrated how to light Bunsen burners.

Oliver squeezed the striker arm across the flint on his sparker. Sparks shot out.

Hmmm, Robbie thought. Looks as if Oliver's done this before.

"Ready?" Mr. Gosling asked the class.

"Yeah!" the kids shouted. Everybody wanted to light fires!

"All right! Everybody practice making sparks. Share your strikers. Switch back and forth."

Robbie watched the kids working with their strikers. Mr. Gosling checked each table for problems. He helped a girl who was scared of her sparker, and showed a boy how to scrape the striker arm against the flint faster.

"Okay, now comes the fun part!" Mr. Gosling declared. "One partner grips the sparker in his or her right hand. The other turns the stopcock at the bottom of the Bunsen burner a half turn. Gas will come out! Be careful and ignite it with your sparker."

Whooshing noises sounded all over the room. The air smelled of gas. Blue flames sprang up everywhere.

Oliver's flame burned fine.

That was when Robbie got an idea. A totally great idea.

He glanced around. Dora floated in an upper corner of the room. She looked bored and tired. Robbie had managed to ignore her whining, so she stopped.

"Hey!" Robbie muttered to his sister. "Watch this!"

He set himself to become visible and audible to Oliver at just the moment he wanted.

Then he jumped into the flame.

His presence made the flame whoosh almost to the ceiling. It sparkled with all kinds of extra colors.

Vwoom! Robbie made himself visible to Oliver.

He stretched first tall and then wide and let his face melt into a skull.

He lifted his arms and waved them at Oliver. His arms were bright gas-flame blue. He could feel his eyeballs glowing.

He mustered his best deep, spooky laugh.

"MOO-HOO WHA-HA HA-HA!" he laughed, looming over Oliver. Blue flames flared over him, flickered up from his fingers.

"OLIVER BOWEN," Robbie bellowed. "I HAVE YOU NOW!"

14

Robbie leaned toward Oliver, eagerly waiting for his terrified shriek.

Oliver frowned.

Not screamed, frowned!

Robbie reached toward him, twitching blue-flame fingers and roaring with evil laughter.

Oliver backed up half a step.

It was the most response Robbie had ever gotten out of him. Maybe, just maybe, the scare was working!

"JUST YOU WAIT, OLIVER BOWEN!" Robbie yelled in his deep, scary voice. He clacked his jawbone.

Oliver yawned.

Yawned!

Any normal kid would have run screaming in terror!

75

Robbie looked around. None of the other kids seemed scared either. Maybe they couldn't see him.

By this time Robbie was feeling pretty feeble—all his energy was going up in smoke!

Oliver raised his hand. "Mr. Gosling?"

"Yes, Oliver?" Mr. Gosling asked.

"Could you help me? My flame is way too high."

Mr. Gosling came and turned down Oliver's Bunsen burner.

Feeling weak and discouraged, Robbie drifted to the floor. He was so tired, he could hardly hold up his head.

"Can we go home *now?*" Dora demanded.

What? She wasn't going to nag him for failing again? She *really* must be sick!

He peered at her. Even for a ghost, she looked thin and transparent.

He gazed down at his own hands. He could see through them.

Neither of them had enough energy to yell boo!

"Later," Robbie mumbled. "I'm too pooped to move."

What an exhausting, weird day, Oliver thought as he stood at his locker. He sorted through his books, figuring out which ones to take home and which to leave at school.

Pencils in the ceiling. Spinning in class. Kids talking about him. And then science class.

Oliver slammed his locker shut. He didn't even want

76

to think about everything that had happened. He just wanted to go home and forget all about this day.

It was late. Most of the kids had already left. Oliver headed for the exit.

That was when he got the weird feeling that someone was watching him.

It felt like a tingle between his shoulder blades. And an itch on his scalp, as if his hair were trying to stand on end.

He turned quickly to look over his shoulder.

There was no one there.

Cut it out, Oliver scolded himself. You're being a jerk.

Maybe all the strange things at school had set him on edge. Because, no doubt about it, he felt very nervous.

Nervous enough to pick up his pace. He clutched his science book and darted through the empty halls.

He hated feeling jumpy. But he couldn't stop the feeling.

There it was, that tingle again in his back!

A wave of prickles over his head.

His stomach rumbled. Not from hunger.

His chest began to tighten. He tucked his book under his arm and prepared to sprint out the door.

Something cold brushed the back of his neck.

Icy cold!

Frigid fingers crept around his neck!

77

15

Oliver almost leapt out of his skin!

He whirled, his heart pounding, his breath coming in gasps. His science book fell to the floor.

Shawn stood in front of him, blinking through his glasses. He looked surprised.

It was only Shawn!

Oliver felt like an idiot.

"Don't *do* that!" he snapped, rubbing his neck.

"Sorry. I—I didn't mean to scare you."

"Scare me? You didn't scare me," Oliver bluffed. "It's just that your hands are freezing cold!"

"Sorry," Shawn said again. He tucked his hands into his jeans pockets.

Oliver's heartbeat finally slowed down to normal. "What are you doing here anyway?" he asked as he picked up his book. "You don't go to Shadyside Middle School."

"I was looking for you," Shawn explained. "I need to talk to you."

"You need to talk to me? About what?" Oliver asked.

Shawn studied the ground. Then he glanced up at Oliver again. He blinked faster now.

"Ghosts," he mumbled at last.

"Ghosts? Man!" Oliver pushed the glass front door open. They stepped out into a dark, blustery afternoon. A few cold raindrops spattered on Oliver's windbreaker.

"Anybody ever tell you you have a one-track mind?" he asked.

"No," Shawn said, trailing after him.

"Well, you do. Ghosts this, ghosts that. Get a life!"

Oliver glanced toward the school yard. He waved to a few kids from class. One or two waved back. Mostly they just stared.

They must have heard about the pencils. And the spinning, Oliver thought.

Together, he and Shawn headed for Shadyside Elementary.

"Oliver?" Shawn began.

"Huh?" Oliver grunted. He had nearly forgotten about Shawn. He was distracted, wondering what tomorrow would be like in school.

"I have to tell you about the ghosts," Shawn

insisted as they reached Nell's school. "This isn't just some dumb story. I have to warn you!"

"Hey!" Nell jumped up from the bottom step, twirling her pink umbrella. "Where have you been? I've been waiting. You promised to walk me to Tracy's house!"

Oliver clapped a hand to his forehead. "I forgot," he said.

"Yeah, well, remember it now," Nell insisted. "Come on!"

"Nell, Shawn and I were—"

"Shawn can come too, but he's got to come now. Tracy said we'd have ice cream. Let's go!" Nell tugged on Oliver's arm.

"For Pete's sake! Why didn't you just go home with Tracy?"

"You *promised* you'd walk me! Mom said you *have* to walk me! And you have to come back to Tracy's house at five and walk me home!"

"Oh, brother," Oliver muttered.

Nell grabbed his hand, something she almost never did unless she really wanted him to do something, or she wanted to embarrass him. "Come *on*. She lives on Melinda Lane. Hurry up."

Oliver glanced at Shawn.

Shawn looked terminally depressed. He shrugged and walked away. "Later," he called over his shoulder.

Oliver let Nell pull him toward the street, but he

still watched Shawn fading into the shadows of the
dark day.

What was so important?

What did Shawn want to tell him about ghosts that
he hadn't already said?

What was going on?

16

Rain poured down for real now.

Robbie sat by the attic window and watched the street. He was still worn out from his trick with the Bunsen burner, but Dora was pretty perky now that they were back in the attic.

Robbie gazed at Oliver trudging up the street through the rain. His hair was plastered to his head, and his jacket looked sopping wet.

The front door slammed as Oliver entered the house.

Robbie drifted downstairs. He watched Oliver take off his jacket and get a towel to dry his hair with.

No one else was home. Mr. Bowen usually worked at home, but today he had a meeting.

The doorbell rang. Grumbling, Oliver went to the door.

Shawn shivered in the rain on the front steps.

How did Shawn always know exactly when Oliver was home? Robbie wondered. Did he keep track of Oliver from his window or something?

"Oh, good!" Oliver smiled at Shawn. "Come on in. You can help me move my desk up to the attic. I've got most of my stuff up there now. Well, except for the bed."

It was true. Oliver had been messing around with their attic a lot in the last few days. Cleaning out the cobwebs, washing away dust, moving furniture around, storing some of it in the crawl space. It was clear to Robbie that Oliver planned to stay.

Shawn blinked behind his glasses. "Is the desk heavy? I don't feel too strong today."

What a weird thing to say, Robbie thought.

"Oh," Oliver replied. "Well, I guess I can wait till Dad gets home. Want to play checkers?"

"Sure." Shawn hung his wet raincoat on one of the hooks by the door.

"I'm going to make hot chocolate first. I'm freezing. You want some?"

"No thanks," Shawn replied.

"You sure? It's the kind with little marshmallows."

"No, really. I'm not thirsty." Shawn followed Oliver into the kitchen.

"Oh yessss," Dora whispered in Robbie's ear, star-

83

tling him. She rubbed her hands together. "I'm going to get that Oliver. I'll make him believe. There's no way I can fail *this* time!"

Oliver carried a mug of hot chocolate into the living room. He set it down on the coffee table. Chocolate-scented steam curled up past his nose, making his mouth water.

"Oliver, I have to talk to you," Shawn said in a serious tone.

Again? Oliver thought. He pulled the coffee table away from the couch and got down the board and the box of checkers from the game shelf.

"Okay, go ahead," he said, opening the checkerboard. He plopped down on the opposite side of the coffee table from Shawn and took a sip of chocolate.

Mmmm! He squished a mini-marshmallow on his tongue.

Shawn took the red checkers and started putting them in the black squares on one side of the board. "I know it isn't safe here, but I have to say something anyway."

"Not safe?" Oliver repeated, mystified. Shawn sounded like someone from one of those dumb old black-and-white spy movies. "What do you mean?"

"No, it's not—not safe here," Shawn stammered. "The ghosts—they . . ."

But Oliver stopped listening. The mug on the coffee

table was shaking. Puzzled, he stared at it. What was going on? An earthquake?

Checkers slid in slow motion toward Shawn. Something bumped Oliver's elbows.

The coffee table was rising off the floor!

It floated slowly up past his eyes.

Oliver stared, his mouth dropping open. Fear pumped through him.

His hot chocolate mug still sat there, steaming gently, on the flying coffee table!

Oliver slapped his palms on the tabletop and tried to push it down. The table began to tilt. He grabbed for the checkers and his mug, but everything slipped away from him.

A second later, *Oliver* rose from the floor.

"Hey!" he yelled. He grabbed frantically at the air.

He was already three feet off the ground. It felt *so* weird! He flapped his arms over his head, trying to force himself down.

It only made things worse. Oliver lost his balance completely. He began to turn slow cartwheels in the air.

This was much worse than spinning on a chair. He was totally out of control!

"The—the—" Shawn stammered. "Oh, no! Nooooooo!" And he rose off the ground too!

Shawn's mouth opened wide in a silent yell. His eyes were huge behind his glasses.

The checkers lifted from the board and twirled around the room.

The table started spinning faster and faster. Oliver and Shawn spun around it in the other direction.

"Whoa!" Oliver cried, trying to reach something— anything! His heart pounded. "No! Stop!"

He couldn't reach the floor!

He couldn't even grab the table!

"Oh, man!" Oliver moaned. The room whirled by him.

He ducked as Shawn's foot nearly caught him on the chin. He glimpsed Shawn's terrified face.

Spinning . . . spinning. . . . He was getting dizzy.

I'm going to lose it, Oliver thought. Toss my cookies.

Then—wham! He fell. He slammed to the floor. He landed right on his rear end.

"Yeeowch!" he yelped. That hurt!

Shawn thudded down right next to him.

A shadow loomed over Oliver.

He glanced up.

Oh, no! His heart stopped beating.

The coffee table!

It was falling right toward him!

"**N**o!" Robbie shrieked. Horrified, he watched the table plunge toward the boys. It all seemed to happen in slow motion. But there was nothing he could do to stop it.

"Ahhhhhhhhh!" Oliver screamed. He quickly rolled toward the couch. The table clonked him on the side of his head.

Robbie squeezed his eyes shut. He couldn't stand it!

Crash!!!

Dora let out a bone-shattering howl.

Then—silence.

Oh, no, Robbie thought. I don't even want to know what happened.

But he had to find out. Slowly, so slowly, he forced his eyes open.

And immediately wished he hadn't.

Dora hovered beside him, her hands covering her mouth. She was trembling.

Robbie glanced at the floor.

Oh, no!

The table must have crushed Shawn! Flattened him! Robbie couldn't even see Shawn's feet poking out. He must have been smashed right into the floor!

This was terrible. Terrible!

They never meant to *kill* anyone!

Especially someone they weren't even trying to haunt!

"What have you done?" Robbie yelled at Dora. "Why didn't you stop?"

"Why didn't you help me?" Dora wailed.

"Help you!" Robbie cried. "You never want me to help you! You always think you can do everything!"

"I know," Dora whimpered. "I thought—but I couldn't—it was just too much all of a sudden—"

"All of a sudden," Robbie moaned. "Why did you drop the boys and *then* the table? Why didn't you drop the table first?"

"Don't you think I wish I thought of that?" Dora cried, her hands shaking. "Oh, Robbie. This is so horrible!"

Robbie hovered over Oliver. Oliver lay crumpled on the floor, his eyes closed. Robbie floated down beside Oliver and knelt next to him.

Was he dead too?

What were they going to do now?

Neither Robbie nor Dora had enough energy left to lift a feather.

What if Oliver were still alive but needed a doctor?

They couldn't even call an ambulance!

And Shawn—no! Robbie didn't even want to *think* about that.

Robbie sat back on his heels and shook his hands. He was so panicked, he didn't know what to do!

Oliver groaned.

He *was* alive!

Robbie heaved a huge sigh of relief.

At least one of them was alive!

"Oh, my head!" Oliver groaned, and sat up. His brain felt scrambled. He peered around.

Rain streaked down the windowpanes. The house was dark except for a couple of living room lights.

Why was the coffee table upside down on the floor?

Oliver rubbed the back of his head. He felt a bump swelling up like an egg just in back of his right ear.

"Ouch," he muttered.

Checkers littered the rug near him. A big pottery mug lay on its side, with a long splash of hot chocolate leading from its mouth across the carpet toward the fireplace.

And the stupid coffee table was upside down!

What happened here? His brain felt slow and sticky.

"Shawn?" Oliver called. Where was Shawn?

He stared at the coffee table.

His stomach clenched.

A foggy wisp of white showed above the bottom of the upside-down table.

Oliver swallowed.

The wisp drifted higher. It solidified into the top of someone's head.

White-blond hair.

The head rose slowly out of the wood of the table.

Pale blue eyes behind red-framed glasses stared right at Oliver.

Oliver clutched his stomach with both hands.

Oh, no. This was bad.

The head rose even higher, followed by shoulders . . . and arms . . . and a torso . . . and the rest of a body.

Oliver bit his lip. He couldn't look away.

This was really bad!

Shawn sat there on the upside-down table, his legs crossed, his hands gripping his knees. He gazed at Oliver.

Oliver stared back. Speechless.

Whoa. No question about it.

Shawn was a ghost.

18

"You—you're a ghost," Oliver whispered, staring at Shawn.

Robbie grabbed Dora's shoulders and shook her. "See what you did?" he screamed. "See what you did?"

She looked dazed. Stunned. No smart comebacks this time!

She killed a kid!

Ghosts weren't supposed to kill anybody. They were just supposed to scare people!

What would happen to them now?

"That's what I've been trying to tell you for days," Shawn told Oliver.

Shawn became more and more solid as he sat there.

"What?" Oliver asked in a faint voice.

"I'm a ghost!"

"What?" Oliver repeated in a louder voice.

"What?" Robbie cried.

"What!" Dora screamed.

"I'm a ghost," Shawn said very calmly. "I've been a ghost for a couple of years."

A couple of years!

Robbie and Dora stared at each other.

So Dora didn't kill Shawn after all! He was a ghost already. Long before Robbie and Dora haunted Oliver.

The table didn't kill Shawn, Robbie realized. You can't kill someone who is already dead!

What a relief!

Wait a second. Robbie's eyes widened. If Shawn was a ghost, then he could see them. All the time. Even when they were invisible to humans.

Robbie remembered Shawn snapping the comic book shut just when Robbie wanted to take a look at it.

What a jerk!

All this time Shawn had known exactly when they were around! And where they were!

"Psssst!" Dora hissed. She beckoned to Robbie.

He followed her into the wall. He edged up inside the wall until he was right behind a portrait of an old man. He peered out the picture's eyes.

Dora eased away. Probably to find her own peephole. Now they could listen without that ghost-intruder seeing them.

"How can you be a ghost?" Oliver demanded. "I can see you. I can touch you. And you aren't even a tiny bit scary."

Robbie held back a laugh.

At least he and Dora weren't the only ghosts having trouble with Oliver!

"Watch this!" Shawn instructed Oliver. He winked out, then reappeared. He held up his hands, raised his eyebrows. "Should I do it again?"

Oliver just sat there with a confused look on his face.

Is he buying it? Robbie wondered. Is he starting to believe at last?

"Or—how about this one?" Shawn rose and walked around behind the TV set. He bent over and disappeared.

Suddenly his face was on the screen!

He opened his mouth.

Wide.

Wider!

So wide, it took up the whole screen, and Oliver was staring right down his throat!

Shawn laughed!

His spooky, echoing voice was so big, it filled up the whole living room.

Inside the wall, Robbie shivered. He had never even *tried* laughing like that. It was pretty scary! Boy, those new ghosts knew how to do stuff old ghosts like Robbie never dreamed of.

Then Shawn stuck his head right out of the TV and made a horrible face.

His nose melted.

His eyes dripped out of their sockets and oozed down his cheeks.

Oozing eyeballs! Robbie bet he could figure that one out. It looked great!

Shawn cackled, but now his voice was as dry as dust.

Then he pulled his head back into the TV and vanished.

A second later he jumped up, back to looking normal. Normal for Shawn, at least. "Get the picture?" he asked Oliver.

"Uh . . ." Oliver still looked confused.

"Admit it. Say it. Now do you believe in ghosts?" Shawn demanded.

Oliver groaned. "I hit my head pretty hard."

"That explains why I can do this?" Shawn sank into the floor up to his waist.

Oliver stared.

"Huh? Does it?" Shawn asked.

He sank into the floor up to his neck, then stayed there, a head staring up from the rug at Oliver. "Does it?"

"No."

"Go on. Say it. Say you believe in ghosts."

94

"Okay. Fine. I do believe in ghosts," Oliver said. He looked stunned.

Finally! thought Robbie.

Finally Oliver caved!

"Good," Shawn said, popping up into the room again.

Oliver bit his lip. "But—how did you—I mean, uh, how did you . . . die?"

"It's a long, horrible story. I don't have time to talk about it right now," Shawn replied. He sat down across from Oliver. "I have something more important to tell you. There are evil ghosts in this house, Oliver. I've seen them."

"Whaaat?" Dora cried from somewhere in the wall.

He thinks we're evil? Robbie wondered. Us?

"You're my friend. I wanted to warn you," Shawn went on. "They're trying to get you, Oliver. That's why they made you fly around the room just now."

"What? What are you talking about?" Oliver asked.

"What do you mean, what am I talking about?" Shawn looked exasperated. He waved his hands around his head. "Flying! You, me, the table, the checkers. Flying around the room! These ghosts are lunatics!"

"Uh," Oliver began to say, feeling the bump on his head. "I don't remember anything about flying."

"What?" Robbie yelled before he could stop himself.

"What?" Shawn squeaked.

Oliver frowned. "I remember coming home from school. You coming to the door. Us setting up checkers. Then I woke up with a bump on my head, and you tell me you're a ghost." Oliver shook his head, then moaned, grabbing the bump. "Ouch! I still don't know why the coffee table's upside down."

Robbie clutched his head with both heads. All that work, all that trouble—for nothing!

Robbie slid through the wall until he could grab Dora's arm. "Come on," he whispered. "Let's go up to the attic."

She nodded.

They floated upstairs.

"I can't believe it!" Robbie cried as soon as he was sure Shawn hadn't followed them. "You majorly messed up! *Again!*"

"Just shut up!" Dora snapped.

"No! No! I never get to say this! You failed! You went to all that trouble, flew stuff around the room, almost killed Oliver, and he can't even *remember* any of it! Oh, *man!*" Robbie paced back and forth, clenching and unclenching his fists.

"This is the worst day of my entire afterlife," Dora wailed.

"That Oliver is the worst kid I've ever seen!" Robbie declared. He pounded his fist on the desk. Fury raced through him like fire.

He paced to the window and then whirled.

Dora stared at him.

Well, maybe she should. Robbie couldn't remember ever feeling so mad!

"We've wasted one great scare after another on that kid!" he yelled. "Okay. That's it. Now he knows about us. He's been warned. No more games! Tonight we are going to work together. And we are going to scare Oliver Bowen to DEATH!"

19

Robbie perched on his old desk. He was still boiling inside. Dora slouched on the armchair, brooding.

Full night darkened the sky.

It took the ghosts a while to work their energy up to any strength at all.

"This will be an all-out scare," Robbie declared. "Everything we're good at, all at the same time! My best howls, yowls, and chains."

"My best shrieks and groans!" Dora agreed. "And I'll use these sheets." She wandered over to a pile of old bedding. "We could start out wearing the sheets, looking like stupid ghosts in the comics, and then wrap him up in them!"

"Yeah!" Robbie exclaimed. "Let's wrap him up so

only his head sticks out! Then, when he can't move, you could do your skeleton dance!"

"I will. I'll do the skeleton dance. And what's more, I'll make that big Doberman fly!" Dora cried.

"The Doberman. That's right!" Robbie felt so excited, he banged into the ceiling. "Let's use the pets. We'll make the animals attack him! What could be scarier than having your own pets turn on you?"

"I'll handle the dog and the cat," Dora decided. "You do the spider."

"I hate spiders," Robbie objected.

"You don't have to touch it," Dora said, sneering. "You just have to make it fly."

"That's the same as touching it."

"Too bad! I called dibs on the dog and the cat first!"

They stuck their tongues out—way out—at each other. Dora looked like a frog about to snap up a juicy fly.

Dora rubbed her hands together. "Let's do it up here," she suggested. "He keeps bringing more stuff up here. And this is our best place. I'll go get the pets."

"Do you think we'll be ready to do it tonight?" Robbie worried.

"I feel pretty strong," said Dora. "Don't you?"

Robbie closed his eyes.

Yes. He could feel strength flowing into him.

This time it would work.

* * *

99

Robbie jumped up the moment he heard the foot-steps on the attic stairs.

Finally!

It felt as if he and Dora had been waiting all night for Oliver to show up.

Spooky was pretty restless. Thunder had curled up to sleep on the dresser, but the dog kept getting up and lunging toward the stairs.

Robbie always managed to scare him back into the room, but it was tiring.

Besides, what if the dog were hungry or thirsty? Robbie didn't like to be mean to animals.

But now, at last, Oliver was coming up the stairs.

Spooky woofed a greeting.

"Shhh," Dora whispered to Robbie. They both melted into the walls.

Oliver arrived at the top of the stairs carrying the terrarium with the tarantula in it.

Perfect!

Shawn followed him into the attic.

Not so good!

Shawn, that traitor ghost who sided with a dumb lifer.

Robbie wasn't sure what powers Shawn might have. So far he hadn't done anything serious—except pretend to be human.

What if he interfered with the Big Haunt?

Oh, well. Why worry? It was too late to turn back now!

Robbie joined his energy with Dora's.

He concentrated really hard. Up, he ordered silently.

Their force was barely visible at first. Spooky's ears poked up. Thunder's tail twitched, then rose straight up.

"Come on. Come on," Robbie murmured. He didn't dare glance at Dora—he couldn't risk breaking their combined force.

With a surge of energy, the cat and dog rose into the air.

We did it! Robbie thought.

The animals looked startled. The cat squirmed and screeched. The dog flailed its front paws, moaning in terror.

The lid popped off the terrarium. The tarantula floated up into the air, all eight legs twitching.

"Okay, now!" Robbie commanded. It tired him, but the struggling animals began to circle in the air.

"Are you nuts?" Shawn yelled over the racket the dog and cat were making. "You crazy ghosts! Oliver, let's get out of here!"

The animals were kind of hard to control in the air. They kept squirming around.

Oliver glanced at the flying animals. He didn't seem bothered at all! He strolled over to the big mirror in the corner.

What is he up to now? Robbie wondered. How can

he possibly ignore pets in the air? Does this kid *ever* act normal?

"Huh," Oliver grunted. He stared at the mirror. He didn't even pay attention to the animals circling over his head.

What could Oliver be staring at? Robbie gazed into the mirror, forgetting to direct the animals. He could feel Dora's concentration slipping too.

The animals slowed and stopped high in the air.

Robbie gasped as he hovered behind Oliver.

Of course he didn't see himself in the mirror—he was in invisible mode. That was normal.

But there was no sign of Oliver either. And Oliver was standing right in front of the mirror.

Oliver had no reflection!

20

Robbie stared at the blank mirror in total shock. He stared so hard, he forgot to concentrate on lifting.

The animals dropped to the floor with a thud.

Thunder and Spooky streaked down the attic stairs as though their tails were on fire!

The tarantula scuttled over to hide under the desk.

"I know you've been worried about those ghosts, and whether they can harm me, Shawn," Oliver said over his shoulder. "But I assure you, that was never a problem."

He grinned, showing all his teeth.

Including long, glistening fangs!

Oliver spun around and stared directly at Dora and Robbie.

"I see you ghosts," he declared. "I've known about you all along. We vampires have the Sight."

Oh, no! Robbie couldn't believe his eyes.

How could this happen?

Oliver took two steps toward Dora and Robbie.

He was the scariest thing Robbie had ever seen!

Oliver smiled. "I've been teasing you, pretending I didn't notice you. I was forcing you to weaken yourselves. But now I've had enough fun and games!"

Oliver licked his lips. His fangs glittered.

"I'm going to drink now. I'm going to drink up the rest of your energy!"

He gave a menacing laugh.

Then he lunged for the ghosts.

"Nooooooo!!" Dora and Robbie screamed, clutching each other.

"Get me out of here!" Robbie shrieked.

With a huge *whoosh,* he and Dora fled through the wall. Robbie vowed to never *ever* look back.

Still smiling, fangs gleaming, Oliver turned to Shawn.

Shawn stared at him wide-eyed, without a single blink.

Oliver took a step toward him.

Shawn shrank back.

"Wh-what are you going to do with *me?"* Shawn asked in a quavering voice.

21

Good question, Oliver thought. What *should* I do about Shawn?

Before he could figure it out though, someone knocked on the door at the base of the attic stairs.

"Come in," Oliver called.

Shawn scurried to a corner. Far away from Oliver. His eyes were twice their normal size.

Mr. Bowen stepped into the attic. "How'd it go, son?" he asked.

"Great, Dad. They're gone!" Oliver smiled broadly. His fangs hung over his bottom lip.

"Good job, Oliver! Congratulations! So I can now certify this house ghost free?"

"Yup."

"Excellent. I'll include that in my next report."

"Yes!" Oliver punched the air.

"What—what are you talking about?" Shawn asked.

Oliver glanced at the terrified ghost.

"My dad works for the Federal Anti-Spirit Task Force," he explained proudly. It had to be the coolest job ever. "He's a specialist in de-haunting houses. Dad's been teaching me how to help him with his work. We moved into this house because we knew it was haunted. And the best method to get rid of ghosts is to scare them more than they scare you."

"You came up with a great plan," Mr. Bowen said.

Oliver beamed. "Thanks," he murmured.

"Have you heard about any more ghosts in the neighborhood?" Mr. Bowen asked.

Oliver peeked at Shawn. Shawn hunched his shoulders and looked even more terrified.

Should Oliver tell his dad about Shawn?

No. No way.

Maybe it was weird for a ghost hunter to have a ghost for a friend. But Oliver didn't care! He liked Shawn. Shawn was fun. Even if he was a ghost.

Besides, what better way to do research?

"Uh—there are lots of rumors," Oliver said. "Shawn's been telling me some of them. He's a valuable local source."

"Oh?" Mr. Bowen studied Shawn up and down.

"And all the kids at school talk about ghosts too,"

Oliver added quickly, so his dad would stop staring at Shawn. "It sounds like there's enough work around here to keep us busy for years. But there aren't any more bad ghosts in *this* house."

"Good. Fine work, and a fine report." Mr. Bowen patted Oliver's shoulder. "This calls for a celebration. Let's go get some ice cream!"

"Okay, Dad. I just have to catch my tarantula."

"That thing got loose again? You know how your mother hates it when that happens. Better catch it right away," Mr. Bowen said. He headed down the stairs.

Oliver listened for the sound of the door shutting at the bottom of the stairs. Then he turned to Shawn.

Shawn was staring at him. "Thanks for not turning me in," he whispered.

Oliver shrugged. "Hey, you're my friend." He pried the fake fangs out of his mouth.

"You mean—you're not really a vampire?" Shawn asked.

"Naw. It was just part of the plan. Pretty good, huh?"

Shawn shook his head in wonder. "Awesome. And you don't really have the Sight?"

Oliver grinned. "Nope! I was just guessing where they were."

"It was great." Shawn paused. "So when they did all that stuff to you, you knew it was happening?"

"Yeah." Oliver laughed. "I bet I drove those ghosts nuts pretending I didn't notice their hauntings."

"You drove them crazy!" Shawn exclaimed. "It was pretty funny. But how—" He nodded toward the mirror.

"I painted part of the mirror with a special goo that doesn't reflect," Oliver explained. "We scared them right out of the house!"

Shawn shivered. "Those two scared me! They knew good tricks."

"Yeah," Oliver admitted. "But that skull popping out of the TV trick was cool too. I wish I could do that."

"Thanks," Shawn said with a grin.

"I wasn't even sure this vampire trick would work." Oliver stared at the fake fangs in his hand. "For one thing, what would a vampire want with ghosts? No blood!"

He and Shawn laughed.

Oliver popped the fangs back into his mouth.

"Besides," he added. "Everyone knows there's no such thing as vampires!"

Are you ready for another walk
down Fear Street?
Turn the page for a terrifying
sneak preview.

R·L·STINE'S
GHOSTS of FEAR STREET ® #24

MONSTER DOG

Coming mid-August 1997

The beast waits for me every day after school.

It hides in the bushes along Fear Street. It licks its teeth. It sharpens its claws.

It waits just for me.

I never know exactly where it will hide. I never know when it will attack.

But I know it's there.

And it wants to get me.

"Once again, Maggie Clark was the only student who managed to get an A on the last three homework assignments." Mrs. Jenkins announced to the class. She beamed at me.

I sank further into my seat. I felt my face grow warm.

"Little Miss Perfect does it again," Billy Smithers whispered behind me. Someone giggled.

Luckily the bell rang. Whew! Just in time. No more embarrassment.

I know Mrs. Jenkins means well, but all her compliments are *killing* me!

Mrs. Jenkins reminded the class to read chapter ten in our science books. All the kids jumped up from their seats and rushed to their lockers. Everyone was thrilled that school was over for the week.

Except me.

Because now it was time to walk home. And I dreaded it.

The beast was waiting.

I trudged through the crowded hallway. I pushed my way to my locker and organized my school books.

Someone shouted my name. "Maggie!"

I turned and gazed past a sea of students. I spotted my best friend Judy right away. She was taller than most of the boys and had bright red hair. Just the opposite of me. I'm kind of short with long dark hair.

I waved at her as she rambled toward me.

"Happy birthday!" Judy greeted me cheerfully. "Ready to go home and open your presents?"

I nodded weakly. Turning twelve was fun. Getting home was the scary part.

"Hey, what's wrong?" Judy asked, seeing my

expression. I could have told her—but I decided to keep quiet. I already had sort of a wimpy reputation. It kind of went with being "Teacher's Pet."

"I wish I didn't have so much homework on my birthday," I complained.

Judy eyed the pile of books in my arms. "Knowing you, you'll knock it all off before dinner. And then volunteer to do extra chores or something."

"Oh, stop." I rolled my eyes. I slammed my locker and turned around. "I'm not that bad." I giggled. "I mean *good.*"

"I think you should forget homework tonight. Just as an experiment," Judy suggested as we headed out of school.

"Then who would explain our science homework to *you?*" I teased. I pushed open the front door of the school building and stepped outside.

The sidewalk was filled with students. We waved good-bye to a group of friends and headed down the street.

"So do you know what you're getting for your birthday? Anything special?" Judy asked.

I smiled. "Something *very* special," I replied.

Judy grabbed my arm. "What? A CD-player? A TV for your room? Tell me!" she insisted.

"Come over for some birthday cake after dinner," I offered. "And I'll show you."

Judy sighed. "Oh, all right," she said. "If you won't tell me now!"

We kept walking. All the other kids turned off onto side streets. My stomach tightened as we approached my street.

Fear Street.

Where the beast lived.

"Well, here you are, birthday girl," Judy called. "See you around seven o'clock!"

I turned toward Fear Street. I took a step forward, then hesitated.

Judy noticed. "What's wrong?" she asked.

I hugged my school books. "Nothing," I mumbled.

I felt my face turn red. For the second time that day.

It was so embarrassing to be afraid. I mean, I just turned twelve. It's not like I'm a baby. I worried that if Judy knew how scared I was, she would think I was a complete wimp.

"Everything's fine!" I declared. I gave her a big smile and a wave. I hoped she believed me.

She did. "All right," she replied. "See you later!"

She turned and crossed the street.

And I was all alone—on Fear Street.

Everything *seemed* calm and peaceful. The sun shone. Birds chirped. Leaves twirled in the trees.

But I knew it was there—waiting for me.

I took a deep breath and hugged my school books.

"Here I go," I murmured to myself. I took a few steps and stopped.

Something rustled in the bushes.

I froze. And stared at the bushes.

The branches snapped. I took a step backward. Something dashed out at me.

A squirrel.

I screamed before I could stop myself. The poor little squirrel jumped in fright and scampered up a tree.

I burst out laughing.

Get a grip, Maggie! I scolded myself. Afraid of a squirrel? How pathetic!

I studied the entire length of Fear Street.

Nothing but trees and grass and sunshine.

I picked up my school books and marched boldly down the street. I glared at every bush I passed.

I expected the beast to jump out at me any second. But it didn't.

"Okay, Maggie," I whispered. "You're halfway home. You don't have to be afraid of that crummy beast. Not anymore."

Then something growled behind me.

I clutched my school books so tightly, my knuckles hurt. Slowly I turned around. My heart raced.

Something moved in the shrubbery near the sidewalk. Something big.

It was him—the beast! I stepped backward. "N-nice boy," I stammered. "G-good boy."

The thing in the shrubs moved.

Then it attacked!

I screamed as the beast lunged out of the shrubbery.

Bullhead!

The biggest, ugliest, meanest dog on Fear Street!

It was coming after me!

I shrieked and ran.

The massive thing snarled and snapped at my ankles. His huge, hideous head bobbed up and down. His sloppy, wet tongue flopped from side to side.

"No, no!" I screamed.

My sneakers slapped against the sidewalk. My long hair flew in my face. I could hardly see where I was going, but I didn't care. I had to get away from the thing chasing me.

Its sharp toenails clicked on the sidewalk behind me. It was getting closer.

I flew forward, even faster. "I'm almost home," I chanted under my breath. "Almost home . . . almost home . . . almost home . . ."

I spotted my house in the distance. The front porch. The oak tree. The white picket fence.

Home!

I glanced over my shoulder as I bolted across the street.

It was right behind me!

I was going to have to dive over the fence. It was my only chance.

I dashed forward and threw my books over the fence. Then I leaped into the air.

Up, up, up, and over . . .

I was halfway over the fence when something tugged at my leg. I shrieked.

It was the beast.

And its jaws were clamped around my ankle!

About R.L. Stine

R.L. Stine is the best-selling author in America. He has written more than one hundred scary books for young people, all of them best-sellers.

His series include *Fear Street, Ghosts of Fear Street* and the *Fear Street Sagas*.

Bob grew up in Columbus, Ohio. Today he lives in New York City with his wife, Jane, his teenage son, Matt, and his dog, Nadine.

R·L·STINE'S
GHOSTS of FEAR STREET ®

1 HIDE AND SHRIEK	52941-2/$3.99
2 WHO'S BEEN SLEEPING IN MY GRAVE?	52942-0/$3.99
3 THE ATTACK OF THE AQUA APES	52943-9/$3.99
4 NIGHTMARE IN 3-D	52944-7/$3.99
5 STAY AWAY FROM THE TREE HOUSE	52945-5/$3.99
6 EYE OF THE FORTUNETELLER	52946-3/$3.99
7 FRIGHT KNIGHT	52947-1/$3.99
8 THE OOZE	52948-X/$3.99
9 REVENGE OF THE SHADOW PEOPLE	52949-8/$3.99
10 THE BUGMAN LIVES!	52950-1/$3.99
11 THE BOY WHO ATE FEAR STREET	00183-3/$3.99
12 NIGHT OF THE WERECAT	00184-1/$3.99
13 HOW TO BE A VAMPIRE	00185-X/$3.99
14 BODY SWITCHERS FROM OUTER SPACE	00186-8/$3.99
15 FRIGHT CHRISTMAS	00187-6/$3.99
16 DON'T EVER GET SICK AT GRANNY'S	00188-4/$3.99
17 HOUSE OF A THOUSAND SCREAMS	00190-6/$3.99
18 CAMP FEAR GHOULS	00191-4/$3.99
19 THREE EVIL WISHES	00189-2/$3.99
20 SPELL OF THE SCREAMING JOKERS	00192-2/$3.99
21 THE CREATURE FROM CLUB LAGOONA	00850-1/$3.99
22 FIELD OF SCREAMS	00851-X/$3.99
23 WHY I'M NOT AFRAID OF GHOSTS	00852-8/$3.99

 Available from Minstrel® Books
Published by Pocket Books

POCKET
BOOKS

Simon & Schuster Mail Order Dept. BWB
200 Old Tappan Rd., Old Tappan, N.J. 07675

Please send me the books I have checked above. I am enclosing $_____(please add $0.75 to cover the postage and handling for each order. Please add appropriate sales tax). Send check or money order--no cash or C.O.D.'s please. Allow up to six weeks for delivery. For purchase over $10.00 you may use VISA: card number, expiration date and customer signature must be included.

Name _____

Address _____

City _____ State/Zip _____

VISA Card # _____ Exp.Date _____

Signature _____ 1146-21